A MYSTERY NOVEL

Beethoven's

TENTH
SYMPHONY

ERIK ERIKSSON

Tate Publishing & Enterprises

Published by Tate Publishing & Enterprises, LLC
127 E. Trade Center Terrace | Mustang, Oklahoma 73064 USA
1.888.361.9473 | www.tatepublishing.com

Tate Publishing is committed to excellence in the publishing industry. The company reflects the philosophy established by the founders, based on Psalm 68:11,
"The Lord gave the word and great was the company of those who published it."

Published in the United States of America

ISBN: 978-1-61739-291-7
1. Fiction: Religious
2. Fiction: General
10.12.03

Dedication

To my father, who had the initial idea for the story and to Beethoven's pearl of great striving.

Author's note:

In this novel the location of a Christian academy on the island of Crete in the Mediterranean is based on the existing Orthodox Academy of Crete at Kolimpari and the nearby sixteenth century Gonia Monastery. However, there are no ties between the author and this academy.

Beethoven Back On Stage

I had been Editor-In-Chief of the *Times of London* for nearly ten years when this business started, and prided myself on knowing words. Yet never, in all that time, had I, JJ Johnson, read such sensational headlines in the write-up of a new symphony played at Festival Hall.

After all, this was not the 1824 premiere of Beethoven's ninth symphony in Vienna when Beethoven was on stage himself. I had read that the deaf Beethoven had to be turned around by one of the soloists to face his audience so he could see their thundering applause and acknowledge their standing ovation. So enthusiastic had been the crowd that the police had to be called in case there was a disturbance. Now *that* was sensational!

I couldn't believe what I was reading in the London newspapers: "A Mystery Symphony from Heaven," "Beethoven Back On Stage," "Beethoven's Tenth Symphony," and "Beethoven's Prophecy." What on earth was going on?

I recalled the look on some of my musician friends' faces when one evening at The Royal Albert Hall I had described the evening's singing as "pretty" and "nice." They knew I was out of my depth. To them I was a philistine, somebody out of touch with music's power to sound the truth of the soul. My answer was 'words are my thing.' But then they would quote Shakespeare's own words against me–*"the man that hath no music in himself…."* My wife Angela told me I would always adjust my glasses or twitch my nose when I met someone who clearly knew more than I did on music or the arts.

Wanting to set me right, they sat down at a piano and straight-a-way composed a simple melody that captured the emotional side of me to a tee. I laughed freely, and acknowledged that I was indeed somehow linked to that melody of musical notes! Yet fifteen minutes later I, a man of words, in the land of the great dramatist himself, could still not string them together to express what had taken them minutes to compose. I wondered why I was so surprised by this. After all, wasn't a painting said to be worth a thousand words? Their simple melody was probably worth a small book. I only had to take one glance at a picture of my children to see the truth of this. No wonder Beethoven wrote that "Music is a more lofty revelation than all wisdom and philosophy." Could the mystery of life really be beyond words?

Putting down my paper that morning after reading the reports about the previous night's concert, the frown on my face must have been unusually bewildering. Lucy, my secretary, looked at me in disbelief. She had never seen me slump into my chair before.

"JJ, are you all right?"

All and sundry called me JJ. I suppose it was easier than "Mr. Johnson, sir," even for those who didn't know me. I wasn't offended, although sometimes it did seem presumptuous to those who knew me well. The word in the office was "The boss is easy to get along with, a problem solver who likes to take charge."

My eye suddenly caught sight of the front page of *The Times* of January 25 1965; actually, an embedded holographic image of that page when you looked towards the top of my office desk.

"Sir Winston Churchill Dies… The Greatest Englishman of His Time… … World Leader in War and Peace"

I knew this had been the first time in the twentieth century that the front page of *The Times* had news on its cover page instead of classified ads. *The Times* had broken with its long-standing tradition to report the news of Churchill's passing along with the highlights of his life on its front page. "But what a story that was!"

I returned to the write-up about last night's concert.

As I read "Astonishing scenes at Festival Hall" (which was one paper's headline on the previous night's concert,) images of the audience jumping up and down and throwing their programs at the conductor paraded before my vision. "Did they boo? Did they yell out in praise?

Throw their hats in the air as happened when Beethoven conducted his ninth symphony in Vienna in 1824? That would be sensational. But could it be true? At Festival Hall here in London, the reserved British?" I started to reflect on my own family and how they would have acted. Then I thought about my wife, Angela, and her family with their proud naval tradition. Angela's elder brother, Edward, had joined the Navy as soon as he could, leaving Angela free to use her sharp, discerning mind where she wanted, in the intelligence service.

I used to tell her that if Conan Doyle had known her, the world would never have known Sherlock Holmes, as he would have been eclipsed by beauty as well as brains.

That these audience scenes could not be true soon crossed my mind. Even if the rumors were true that the audience had seen Beethoven hovering over Sir Henry Malcolm helping him to conduct, London concertgoers would not react like this. They would never have jumped up and down in their seats during a concert at Festival Hall—in Vienna perhaps, but certainly not here. I couldn't see any of these things happening here. But then what was behind this furor?

I started to read *The Times'* own music critic, Anthony Sargent, expecting, perhaps even hoping to find his normal, scathing comments wherein he lambasted anything and anyone new. This would have reassured me that it was indeed just another concert, and that I, albeit a musical philistine, was still of sound mind! My nose started to twitch. Sargent could be quite annoying.

"... Last night's first performance of a new symphony by someone called Beynon evoked the most astonishing scenes at The Royal Festival Hall never seen before, certainly in my lifetime. At the end of each movement there was a deathly silence as if the audience had been stunned or knocked senseless. There was no rustling of programs, nor the usual buzz of movement. People stared blankly at one another as if something unbelievable had taken place. Some could be seen rubbing their eyes. At the conclusion of the work, once again there was a deathly silence as if everybody had been struck down and rendered speechless. For about fifteen seconds there was a profound vacuum as it were, as though everybody had held their breath, only to be broken by a tremendous burst of clapping and shouting and calls for the composer, who was not present. Sir Henry Malcolm, the conductor, in a voice breaking with emotion, told the audience that Beynon, the composer, was ill, and went on to add that he could say no more as the music had so moved him that he had to retire. Those seated closest to him said that Sir Henry had turned pale, as though he had seen a ghost from the past that brought unwanted tidings.

At the rehearsal in the afternoon, the orchestra had been so intrigued that they were asking the most extraordinary questions of Sir Henry. Two or three of the violinists had even suggested that this was Beethoven, but nothing they had ever played before. Sir Henry had replied that he, too, was very puzzled. He hinted at a mystery behind its composition, to which members of the orchestra were ready believers, seeing with their own eyes that Sir Henry himself was decidedly pale and clearly not himself. Most were apprehensive of playing this "mystery symphony" again that evening. They wanted to because it was truly magnificent, sounding like Beethoven at his best. But equally, they did not want to, since it made them feel as though their end was nigh. It was deeply personal.

"Yes, yes, yes. Now, where are your scathing comments Anthony? Let's cut to the chase." But I couldn't find any scathing comments. Instead I read:

"I will not even attempt to comment on the musical content. This work is beyond any criticism of mine."

I jumped out of the chair in one swift movement. "This is unbelievable."

"And this is from you, Anthony? I can't believe this."

JJ's face was a picture of utter amazement, as he read again this astonishing review from the Times' own music critic. He could not fathom this. This was a first if he ever had seen one.

"You always slam new composers in the most vitriolic fashion, and most musicians of the day have writhed under your reviews. One opera manager had even told him, "If I could, I would bar Mr. Sargent from here as his presence is enough to send the sopranos and contraltos into near hysteria. The men, well, they just start swearing quite freely.'"

I understood this opera manager very well, but couldn't say so. Music lovers bought the Times just in anticipation of his next scathing comment!

I dialed Sargent, waiting impatiently as the ringing tone went on interminably. Finally a grumpy voice answered,

"Speaking."

"Huh, who's speaking?"

"Who the devil do you think?" came back a sharp voice. "You dialed me, didn't you?"

"Is that you, Anthony?"

"Of course it is. What do you want, JJ?"

"What do I want? What's all this stuff you've written about the concert? You of all people won't comment, why not?"

"If somebody put a newly discovered sculpture by Michelangelo in your hand and said 'How do you like that?' What would you say?" demanded Sargent.

"Are you serious?" I asked.

"Of course I'm serious, you old philistine; this music is out of this world."

I adjusted my glasses, "Why didn't you say so?"

"Because, you old—" he wanted to say "goat," but didn't. "I need time to study it."

"When are you going to do that then?"

"When am I going to do that? What do you think I've been doing since about twelve o'clock last night? I've been listening to the recording over and over again and frankly I just cannot understand how Beynon, whoever he is, wrote this. If you promise not to say I am insane, I'll tell you now only one man could have written it and he's been dead around 180 years."

"You mean … ?"

"I mean Beethoven, now say I'm mad—because I will agree with you. The question is, did Beynon get it from Beethoven? And if so, how? Goodbye." And with those words Sargent rang off.

"Well I'll be damned."

"Lucy, get me a recording of last night's concert at the Festival Hall as quickly as you can."

"Where do I get that, JJ?"

"You know where to pick up your paycheck don't you? Get moving. This is urgent. Get Sir Henry Malcolm on the phone, too."

Five minutes later I heard, "Will you dial him yourself, JJ? When I asked him to hold on, he said 'Why should I? Let your man hold on!' and banged the receiver down. I tried again explaining who wanted him and he said 'Don't waste my time girl!'"

"All right, Lucy. What's come over the musicians? They're all so touchy this morning. What's the number? Thank you." I got queer sounds and squeals suggesting I was being connected to outer-space, but after three further attempts I was greeted by a bawling, "Who is it? What do you want?" In the background an orchestra was playing.

"This is Johnson, Editor-In-Chief of the *Times*, Sir Henry. I'd like to speak to you about that concert last night."

"Ask Sargent. I see he's written about it in your rag," replied Malcolm.

"I have. But for someone usually so caustic about new music he's simply tongue-tied and really he's made the most astonishing remarks I've ever heard."

"Oh, did he? What was that?" asked Sir Henry Malcolm.

"He said I'd say he was crazy because in his opinion the music of that symphony could only have been written by a man who died about 180 years ago—Beethoven—and then said he'd been listening to the recording over and over again since midnight. You conducted the concert last night, can you say anything?"

Sir Henry wondered if he had conducted it.

"My dear man, I've been listening to the recording ever since I got home too. Goodbye." And with that, Sir Henry rang off, leaving me hanging and holding my breath.

"Well, I'll be double-damned." Slamming the receiver down, I shouted for Lucy, who entered rather timidly.

"Well, where's that recording?"

"I'm sorry, JJ, but I've been on to three agencies who record all broadcasts and they all say we will have to take our turn; they've been getting requests from all over the country and the continent for copies, and with luck we might get one by tomorrow morning."

"Get me the BBC musical head. His name is Thurston—put him through to me as soon as you can."

I sat there drumming my fingers on the table, gazing perplexedly at the wall opposite. Some time later the phone rang. I pressed the speakerphone button to talk.

"Oh, hello Jack. JJ here. What the hell's this musical mystery all about? Something extraordinary happened at Festival Hall last night and I can't get a word of sense out of Malcolm, or indeed Sargent. What's it all about? I know it's a new work, but we've had lots of those and never have I known Sargent to be cagey. He usually gives new composers hell—that's if he ever mentions them, but he just refuses to comment. What do you say?"

There was a long silence only broken by me yelling: "Jack, are you still there?"

"Yes, I'm here and frankly I don't know what to say. I was at the concert because Malcolm told me it would be worth my while attending. He said he thought I'd probably share his shock. You know I studied at The Royal Academy of Music under him."

"Yes, yes, but where's the catch, what goes on? Who's this chap Beynon the composer? For goodness sake, I get the impression the whole blasted musical world is in a state! What's this Beynon done to cause all this uproar? Other people have written music, Elgar, Britten, Vaughan-Williams, Tippett. I can't even get a recording of it—why?"

"Well, JJ, most of the authorities I've been on to are utterly mystified not only by the music which they say is fit to rank with any great work but also by the interpretation put on it that suggests, as Lunn the leader put it, 'a message from another world' and, don't laugh, that's exactly what I think. I'll go even further and say it could be Beethoven's Tenth Symphony. Yes I know—I am crazy too. Beynon is a harmony teacher at the Royal Academy and, until yesterday, quite undistinguished. This music is an indictment of Man, and a warning. I can tell you one thing. Sir Henry was as white as a sheet at the end of the performance so he must have got it, too. Goodbye."

"Got what?" But I was left hanging in the air, yet again, not something to which I was accustomed before this business began. Gazing blankly at the phone, before slowly putting the receiver back on the cradle, I remembered that a handwritten manuscript of some Beethoven work had been found in a Pennsylvania seminary library and sold at Sotheby's for nearly two million. Could there be a connection with Beynon and this new mystery symphony? But how could this be? This was not an old manuscript just discovered. This chap Beynon composed it, not Beethoven, mystery or no mystery.

There was a knock at the door. In walked Laxton, the features editor.

"Ah, Larry, just the man I want to see. I can't get a line on this concert last night. Do you know anything about it?"

"Well, JJ, I heard you were foraging around so I've been busy, but I can't get much further. Armstrong at the Academy says Beynon is very ill and can't be seen and when I asked if one could get the score he said Beynon gave it to Sir Henry, and it's still in manuscript form, with the injunction that it was not to leave his possession. Sir Henry won't allow anyone to take the music away to study. He just collected it again personally after every rehearsal. Even the four sopranos had to pretty near sight read a fairly tricky part in the slow movement. He simply told them 'If you can't read it I'll get someone who can.' As you know, they were lovely and someone even said 'angels,' and once again mystery piles on mystery."

"Look here, Larry, we've got to get to the bottom of all this. How do we start? I'm convinced that Sir Henry knows a great deal more about this, otherwise he would never have put it on at Festival Hall. He just refuses to say anything. We could try Armstrong the Principal at the Royal Academy of Music—he must know something? Wait, let me think…"

Okay, this will have to be a proper investigation. The experts can examine the music, but I want the story. There's something most unusual about this. Send in the inspector, he's got a flair for getting people to talk. He'll find out what they've all got. After all, he foiled that attempted terrorist attack on the underground here before 9/11 in New York. Some at The Yard even say that if he had not been let go, the July 7, 2005 terrorist attacks here in London would never have succeeded. He can get to work on it."

"Right ho," said Leyton, "but he's no music lover."

"I don't want people writing about inner meanings and emotive performances. Some are now calling this 'Beethoven Back on Stage.' I don't know if this means Beethoven was seen during the performance. But I want someone who will dig up the facts and get us the story. That's Lewis."

I suddenly noticed again in my desk what *The Times* had said following Churchill's passing.

I wondered what *The Times* of 1827 had written following Beethoven's death. I checked out the archives.

The Times of April 19 1827 reported:

"The file of carriages at the funeral of Beethoven, at Vienna, was said to be endless. A little more attention to him on the part of the owners, while living, would have been more to the purpose…"

A similar sentiment had been expressed in a letter to the editor from The London Philharmonic Society the day before:

"I cannot help feeling much surprise that the Emperor of Austria, who professes to be such a patron of music, could have allowed this accomplished veteran to be lingering in misery at Vienna, without affording every possible assistance and comfort to him."

More searching and I discovered that the last spoken remembrances of the dying Beethoven were to thank The Philharmonic Society of London for their great gift, and indeed the whole British nation.

But what was this great gift from the Philharmonic Society of London that warranted such grandiose thanks?

The Times of April 5 reproduced an article from *The Austrian Observer* of March 22 published four days before Beethoven's death. The gift was explained:

"... *M. Moschelles hastened to lay the case before the Philharmonic Society, which unanimously resolved at a very numerous meeting to afford him, not only for the moment, but in future, all the assistance of which he might stand in need. ... It is difficult to describe the deep emotion with which Beethoven received the information of this generous action; and if his worthy friends in London could have been witnesses of it, they would have felt themselves amply recompensed for their considerate liberality ... "*

More searching in the archives and other commentaries and I found that Beethoven had indeed expressed his thanks for this gift just days before his passing:

"When I get better I will go to London and compose a grand symphonic overture for my friends the English."

Then, when realizing that he would not recover, Beethoven asked that a letter of thanks be sent to the Philharmonic Society of London on his behalf.

"Tell them: They have comforted me in my last days, and even on the brink of the grave, I thank them and the whole British nation for the great gift. God Bless Them."

Putting these archives down, I wondered if the comedy or drama was really over, as some reported Beethoven to have said just before he died. From what the experts were now saying it looked like a new chapter was beginning with his friends, the English. Beethoven had indeed written out a few bars for his tenth symphony while still alive. Could it be that he was now using this Beynon fellow to get it all down on paper to thank his friends in London?

Was the truth really beyond words? My head started to pound and my nose twitch as thought after thought paraded onto the stage of my mind in quick succession.

"Good Lord, what if this 'mystery symphony' really is Beethoven's thanks to the whole British nation, and just as he expressed it before he died! It wouldn't be the first time that someone's dying wish had come to pass after their death. Could the next world and this one be connected?"

I knew the inspector would do his best. And I thought we would get to meet those who could help; this "mystery symphony" would likely see to that. But would the inspector be up to getting this story? As far as I knew he wasn't psychic!

Like Napoleon when choosing his senior officers for a campaign, I knew that to pursue this investigation successfully we would benefit from having someone who clearly carried Lady Luck on their shoulders. Would the inspector prove to be lucky? Time was going to tell, but only right at the end of the investigation.

The Inspector Called In

Inspector Michael Lewis had been "let go" by Scotland Yard. It didn't sound like Lady Luck for a cop to be fired by Scotland Yard! Yet after his trouble there I made him a generous offer to join *The Times* as our Chief Investigator, which he accepted. His honesty and commitment to the truth during his trouble at The Yard had been impressive, as well as his ability to dig it up quickly.

Some of my contacts at the home office told me that he had been "too good" at his job and politically naïve at the same time. I sometimes wondered if he had left Scotland Yard at all. He was in constant touch with his old bosses there still giving them information acquired at the *Times* that he knew would "help them in their investigations." He was clearly an inspector at heart whether working for the police or not. We even addressed him as the "inspector."

Before hiring Lewis, I had checked him out thoroughly. Since his father had been in the police force, I had no difficulty in finding out his family background and what made him tick. I quickly learnt that his father certainly didn't see him as lucky. There was clearly discord in their relationship. I shared with him what I had found out. Appreciating my honesty, Michael filled me in.

" ... After graduating from university, JJ, I followed in my father's footsteps and joined the police via their college. I inherited one priceless gift from my father—how to understand my fellow man and the criminal mind. He taught me how to place myself in the other person's shoes, and then to use keen deductive reasoning coupled with a basic knowledge of human frailty. This allowed me to draw conclusions that invariably proved to be correct. I worked hard and rose quickly to the rank of inspector in the C.I.D, but in a division separate from my father. I enjoyed my work and was then transferred to Security Services and MI5 where I helped to prevent that pre-9/11 terrorist attack on London."

But on my twenty-first birthday I had not followed my father. I had formally disappointed him. I declined his invitation to become a Freemason. Looking back, I think I was happy to do so. My father's comment that many police officers were masons did not sit well with me. In fact, it drove me to apply to the police college on my own merit. I saw Freemasonry as a social club and a remnant of an unscientific past with rituals and secret handshakes, despite my father telling me that the emperor Napoleon had been one of their bigwigs. My father kept a picture of the emperor hanging prominently in his study as though we were all supposed to venerate the man. Whoever had painted this Napoleon was clearly trying to show the will-power that came through his eyes. Since Beethoven and his music was my father's passion, I wondered why my father had not put up a picture of Beethoven on his study wall instead, showing beautiful music streaming out from the composer's head. The emperor and my father had at least one thing in common. My father's Masonic activities had often resulted in my mother being left alone, so I did not listen when he expounded on its benefits and what he did in it and why. As for Napoleon, he was always away making war somewhere."

"Was that all you judged your father on, Michael, that he had left your mother alone when he went to the masons? Surely not!"

"Well, no, you are right, JJ. I hate to admit it, but I blamed my mother's sickness on my father's heavy smoking. What made it so bad was that he smoked in bed. Even worse, JJ, I realized later on that I had looked down on my father for not paying the bills on time. Money was the big issue in our house. You see, my parents were always arguing about it, and the situation was never dealt with or resolved."

I said nothing to this revelation since I could see that Michael was content with the idea that his father was the villain. I wondered if his mother did not have this view of his father first, but said nothing. It was not surprising that he had come into conflict with the authorities at Scotland Yard. I suddenly caught my breath.

"Will I also want to get rid of him?"

I looked away to hide my surprise. But then I remembered that Michael had been sent to private schools. No wonder money was an issue in his house! Was he that ungrateful?

Michael resumed his story:

"Well, I got married myself at twenty-one, JJ, and moved out of the house. I knew the family and relatives said that I was happy to leave and be my own boss, and there was truth in this. Soon after we married, I saw that my wife and mother would not get along. My wife seemed to object that I wanted to see my mother and check up on her. It just got worse and worse, and we later separated."

My father had advised me to wait before proposing marriage, but of course I didn't listen. Shortly after, my mother suddenly died of a stroke when I was away at the police academy. This family tragedy was a wakeup call for all of us, not knowing how long anyone would live."

After a year or so, my father found himself a lady friend who was a Jehovah's Witness, and a senior civil servant in the government. They had many "lively" discussions on religious matters since my father was more mainstream in his religious thinking. But she loved Beethoven too, and this helped to smooth over their differences. She was a helpful and smart lady who did a lot for my father after my mother's death. I learnt from her, JJ, that people can still be honest, good, and caring, even if their religious views seem weird."

"To have learnt that Michael at a young age, is really quite something. There, you are decidedly lucky."

"Well, a year or so later my father collapsed one day and was dead the next. At his cremation I remember sitting down watching his coffin move into the fire. I asked myself 'How are you, Daddy?' I saw a picture of my father's body lying on a slab of marble. A large blade came down and rent his body asunder. Then a little bird flew up into the sky where Beethoven was playing. I took this to mean that his soul had been freed from the body and was going to where his heart lived, to Beethoven and his music. My father would have loved that. Strangely, I could see the notes too. They had their own different colors as well."

"Michael, here you really surprise me. Some folks would say this was an amazing experience. But you describe it in such a matter of fact way as though that's just the way it was."

"Well, that is just the way it was, JJ. It was the answer I got to my question. I knew I would get an answer. I always have."

I wondered how Michael and this unfinished business with his dead father would play out. I had never seen him as religious, yet there was clearly a side of himself that he took for granted and trusted, despite being a no-nonsense detective. I didn't know about Lady Luck, but I realized that the "inspector" had one thing going for him. He was good at getting answers to questions that most folks never asked.

"As you know, JJ, I have not remarried, although I have had several girlfriends. To be honest, I am a little wary of marriage and commitment. My family had its issues, and it's clear that I have yet to come to terms with them."

"Perhaps, then, Michael, it's a good thing that you have not remarried, and that you did not have children. But then your marital problems must have been completely overshadowed by that horrendous spy-ring business and the political fallout from it that brought you to *The Times*. After all, you were the "hot potato" at The Yard that nobody senior wanted."

"You're right, JJ. That I was in over my head only struck me when it was too late. After the pre-9/11 attempted terrorist attack on the London underground was foiled, I was riding high, as you can imagine. Even my father's congratulations sounded genuine. When I was assigned afterwards to work on that commercial spy-ring business, I did wonder why they chose me when others more experienced were available."

I was warned to be careful but I wanted to solve the case and show what I could do. Why not? It was a great opportunity for a young detective. Several of the Russian oligarchs were players behind the scenes with copies of prototypes finding their way to Iran and the East, as well as to Russia. The problem was that none of the big manufacturers proved to be completely honest in this affair. It never occurred to me that some in our government already knew about this. I sensed trouble coming but did not want to believe it. I just thought that if I were true to myself, all would be okay. My father had taught me that...My father was wrong!"

Maybe, I thought, but there was a price to be paid for everything. The question was, had he already paid the price, or was his payment still to come?

"Well, here, Michael, I saw matters more clearly than you. My wife and I saw the efforts that were made to discredit you when you refused to drop the investigation. That was when *The Times* realized you would take the fall and need support. We decided to be frank with our reporting so that public opinion would make it impossible to whitewash even the highest in the land. Senior government officials were decidedly uncomfortable when your name was mentioned. They urged Security Services to have you removed—"transferred," they called it. They feared that they might become the subjects of your next investigation!"

This must have been very hard for you, Michael, without your father and wife's support. After all, you were digging up the truth brilliantly with a most promising career in front of you, only to be made the scapegoat and lose your job."

Michael gave no indication of how hard it was for him. Was he covering it up or did he handle this better than most? I wondered if his trouble at Scotland Yard had been his nemesis, payback for judging his father, a policeman himself. Didn't they call it karma—what goes around comes around? It sounded like the spiritual version of Newton's third law–for every action there is a reaction. The only question was if there was more to come.

"You know, JJ, I suspect they got at my father as well, since he made it perfectly clear to me that he thought I had brought this all on myself by not heeding the advice from my superiors as well as from him. But I suspect my father would have blamed me anyway. I thought this was dandy coming from him. As you might imagine, he and my wife got on very well!"

Such was the quiet, watchful man in his early forties who crossed the threshold into my office in anticipation of a new and different assignment. And different it certainly was going to be, for all of us. As I watched him walk in with his characteristic gait of pursuing a crime, I wondered what simple musical melody my musician friends would have composed for him. I didn't know, but I did know one phrase that described him well—"still waters run deep."

I wondered if something in the "mystery symphony" would resonate with him.

"Well, Michael, have you read up all the papers about that concert last night?"asked JJ, looking the inspector up and down to see if he could get an answer to his question.

"Yes, just a little, but what's it all about, JJ?"

"Now you are asking. Do you know anything about music? I mean the classics, you know, what some musicians call 'them ops.'"

"Not a darn thing really. I like the old raz-ma-tazz, Glenn Miller, and so on. Concertos and symphonies just pass me by. What's all the mystery about?"

"You've read Sargent's bit in our paper today? Well, every musician and critic in Europe and now America is asking about that work played for the first time at Festival Hall last night. No one will talk rationally and the composer Beynon doesn't seem to be available. The strange thing is that two great musicians have said that only Beethoven could have written it. You have heard of him, haven't you?"

"Of course I have," said Michael, sounding indignant at my presumption. "My father's passion was Beethoven. But Beethoven's been dead for a long time now."

"Actually, Michael, 180 years to be exact."

"All right, all right. But what's all this to do with me?"

"Just this, Michael: Sir Henry Malcolm has got the music. It's in manuscript form and I can't even get a copy of the recording because hundreds of people from all over the world are lining up for it. I believe we've just got to wait. This composer chap Beynon is something at the Royal Academy of Music but that's all I know. I want you to trace him and get the whole story. There's a lot that needs explaining. That's your job. Never mind the strictly musical matter. I want you to attend to the factual and practical. Keep in touch."

"Right," said the inspector as he made for the door, looking bewildered with his new assignment.

Lucy looked up and smiled brightly as Michael walked towards her mumbling, "I'm a detective, not a ghost buster."

"Hello, Michael."

"Hello, Lucy," replied Michael warmly. Is Sargent in?"

"No, he's at home. Snapped my head off and said he's cutting his phone off so that he can listen to some music. Even Sir Henry Malcolm bawled JJ out. I don't know anything about music but they've all gone crazy today. And Keith Miller, who nearly lives at Festival Hall, and as you know, writes our sports stuff, is walking round with a decidedly puzzled look on his face and shaking his head at something."

"Thanks, Lucy. I think I'll go and have a talk with him." And with that Michael smiled at Lucy and walked towards the huge writing room of *The Times*.

As he entered, he eyed Miller, suggesting to him that he would like to have a chat over a pint. Nodding, Keith Miller joined him and minutes later they sat down in the "Mitre" after getting their drinks.

"I'm told, Keith, you're a 'Beethoven fanatic,' to quote one of your pals. Is that so?"

"Well, I suppose so. Even my daughter Elizabeth gets impatient with me over it and she's quite a passable player studying at the Royal College."

"You're just the chap I want to see. Were you at the concert last night at Festival Hall?"

"Oh, so that's it. Yes, I was, why?"

"What's the mystery? Who's Beynon? Why has the chief told me to get a story? I don't know what the story is supposed to be about. I'm an inspector, not a psychic."

Miller sat staring into space for such a long time that Michael got impatient. "Well?"

"I can tell you who Beynon is, that's easy. But commenting on the concert, I don't know. I've never heard anything like it or seen a musical audience so stunned. The silence was devastating and was broken by almost hysterical cheering. Then the conductor, Sir Henry, looked at the audience, spoke his little piece to the orchestra, who also looked stunned, and walked off after the librarian had handed him all the manuscript parts taken from the music stands. He didn't even bow or shake hands with the leader."

"I know all this, but why? Is this some devil music or what?"

"Don't be a bloody fool, Michael."

"Oh come on Miller, for goodness sake put me in the picture. Obviously it's affected you, too. Give me a reason."

"Well, are you musical at all?"

"My father was, but not me. Who's Beynon?"

"He's one of the teachers at the Royal Academy—harmony and piano. Matter of fact, he's my daughter's teacher. Come to think of it, she said the other day that he's been acting very strangely lately."

"That's a lot of help. What about this concert now?"

"It's very difficult to try to explain something of this nature to someone who says he knows nothing about it."

"Look Miller, I'm begging you now—try to help me understand—I don't mean technically, I understand this music goes beyond that and I've no doubt old Sargent will attend to all that in due time."

"I'll try, then, but I'm no authority. And for heaven's sake never quote me."

"Go on. I'm starting to wonder if I've missed something."

"Very well," said Miller to Michael, looking as though he was speaking to someone far off instead of just a few feet away.

"Forget all about pretty music or stuff specially written for operas or overtures and so on. We must deal with great music, or what I call 'absolute music.' Like great poetry, it applies anytime, anywhere. It's emotive, it's not picture painting. The effect on listeners can be quite different and no one can say just what the correct interpretation is.

Beethoven probably was the greatest in this emotive field. While you and I would curse, he would go to the piano and literally say it in music."

"And all this leads to last night?"

" In a most shattering way. You see, Beethoven wrote nine symphonies, the last being perhaps *one* of the greatest if not *the* greatest symphony ever written. It is not an easy piece for sopranos to sing, yet is really powerful and seems to approach the very doors of heaven. A sequel to it would be something, likely a message from very heaven itself. After Beethoven's death, a sketch or outline of a tenth was found. Nobody can really say what it would have been like, despite what's been developed. Then last night this colossal work by an unknown composer is played and it carries all the hallmarks of Beethoven at his greatest. This chap Beynon had composed one or two small pieces used for examinations and so on but never a symphony or sonata. That isn't the mystery so much as what the message says. To my mind, and apparently to others too, it's an indictment of man and a warning, and there you are. I'll say no more. You tackle the experts."

"I see; or should I say I'm blessed if I see? Well, I've got to get the story. I suppose I had better go and see Beynon, though I am told he's not well. Perhaps I could start with Armstrong, the Principal of the Royal Academy ... "

"Yes, good luck. I look forward to reading your story."

"Thanks for your help. I've got a lot of listening and reading to do before I can hope to know what has caused this furor." The inspector recalled that one evening he had visited one of his father's friends who had greeted him at the door with 'Sh-h, Beethoven's seventh you know.' He then had calmly conducted the music until the end of the symphony before taking up the duties of host.

Thinking of this made Michael a little sad that his father was not alive to join him. He knew his father would have loved to be involved in checking out this mystery symphony. He could have given him lots of pointers. But then, Michael knew his father would have insisted on his seniority being in charge, and there was the rub of it.

A little later, Michael came to the conclusion that before talking to people like Armstrong and Malcolm it would be a good idea to get some inkling of what it is that can grip those devotees to the exclusion of everything else. He should have known the answer to this since his father fell into this category, but he didn't.

He decided he would telephone his old musician friend David Martin, and arrange to pop round in the evening to see him.

Michael had first met David during his Police College days when David's sister and he had been in the same class together. He had gotten to know the whole Martin family and found them all delightful. They were always so welcoming. David had a keen, inquiring mind and also had a father in the police force. He had a degree of humility coupled with brilliance that always impressed Michael. After his marriage, David had become a practicing Christian.

David was delighted to see me and welcomed me warmly but expressed some surprise at my request for enlightenment on a subject in which I had previously shown a complete lack of interest, if not actual tolerance.

"Well, David, I've got to unravel a mystery which is really quite beyond my understanding. It concerns music, classical music. I take it you've read the newspapers about that concert the other night. My chief has told me to investigate the mystery surrounding the new symphony written by this chap Beynon. The critics aren't saying anything and you probably know what Sargent's like writing about new works: even I've read his scathing remarks. Sir Henry won't say much and one or two music lovers are cagey and puzzled. What was most astonishing was Sir Henry's behavior at the end of the symphony and the audience's sort of frozen reaction for quite some time, and then the fantastic applause. On top of all this, I'm told— or it's hinted—that no living man could have written it. So I'm here to ask you, a musician and an historian, just what gets a man so worked up, and what you make of this, as someone called it, the 'Tenth.'"

Martin sat for a long time staring at the wall with a faraway, concentrated look and was finally jolted back to reality by my somewhat terse "Well, David?"

"Michael, you've posed a thousand questions. Ask me why Shakespeare is so revered or Da Vinci or Michelangelo. What's the answer? To some extent these are questions for the esoteric, but with a little effort one can come quite easily to differentiate between the first rate and the third rate. The great men set the standard. They were original. Their work was significant. Usually they were years ahead of their time. They perfected the forms of the past, devised new ones which, at the time, were fiercely opposed and criticized by their contemporaries."

"Yes, all right, David, I get that—but come to Beethoven. He's the man I must understand."

"Yes, Michael, you're asking me to explain a genius. Handel, Mozart, Haydn, Schubert, and Bach were all geniuses whose works will stand for all time; but Beethoven went far beyond that. He roughed up the pretty and attractive music. He put red blood into it. It got under people's skins, and they suddenly realized his music was a catalyst to their deep emotions, something set them going; they couldn't explain themselves. Put on almost any slow movement, play it half a dozen times. If it's new to you, you'll find yourself wondering what Beethoven's been saying to you."

Michael found it difficult to relate to any of this. His face showed it. He looked totally blank. He could not imagine sitting through what his father had listened to just to wonder what Beethoven was trying to say to him. His father had often put on Beethoven which he had overheard many times. It hadn't done anything for him.

David walked over to a bookcase and picked up a book and paged through it until he found what he was looking for.

"Michael, listen to what Wagner said about Beethoven:
'*Who does not hear the Redeemer's word when listening to the Pastoral Symphony? And thus these wonderful works preach repentance and atonement in the deepest sense of a divine revelation…*'"

Michael's expression suddenly changed, from one of disbelief to interest as he turned to look David straight in the eyes, and then walked around the room with that characteristic gait of his.

"Wow, David, a divine revelation? What do you say about that?"

This was the first time that David had seen Michael show interest in anything to do with classical music. He wondered if it wasn't something else.

"Well it makes me think of modern-day near death experiences where the individual experiences being drawn up through a tunnel towards a realm of rapture and light that is so appealing and beautiful they don't want to come back."

"Go on David, this sounds interesting."

"My wife's brother, Michael, was struck by lightning and knocked 'out' of his body with a most profound spiritual experience. He didn't want to come back. Before this near death experience he wasn't interested in music. Now, he is almost consumed by the beautiful music that he hears in his head. Talking with him set me off on my own spiritual path."

Michael had never heard his father say anything like this.

"Wow, are you saying that Beethoven had similar experiences? Wait. Let's leave that for the moment."

Michael remembered that JJ wanted him to stick to the hard facts of this 'mystery symphony.' He knew Sargent, as music critic for the Times, would take care of the rest.

"Can you say, David, what is the cause of all this controversy? What's it all about?"

"Michael, I'm a musician, yes, but not a Beethoven specialist, nor a famous conductor of Beethoven of vast experience like Sir Henry. Are you asking me to express a view about a new work that I heard? I was at Festival Hall that evening."

David walked up to the bay window and started looking at the cloudy sky as though to clear his thoughts.

"Let me think. You'll have to have some understanding of the ninth symphony, and here I'm sticking my chin out.

To me, the first movement has always signified 'Destiny;' something like Michelangelo's frescoes on the Sistine ceiling. It's as if it were covering our lives from the creation to our final destiny. Then the second—sheer exuberance, the third, love—and I mean love of mankind—not erotic love, and finally sheer joy, with the gates of heaven opening. You've got to hear it, say twenty or thirty times and then you may, and I say *may* understand it."

Michael thought that sheer exaggeration, if not hyperbole for his benefit, but then realized that David was not joking.

"That's powerful stuff, David. I wish I could have found that out for myself, but go on. What now?"

"Well, Michael, this symphony the other night appeared to me to be the sequel to the ninth and that's plain nonsense. Yet it had all the hallmarks of Beethoven about it. Not only that... There was a clear message or a warning that catastrophe was around the corner. I cannot explain myself because I came away feeling as if the world was about to disintegrate. If you can imagine Exodus in the Bible put to music, that's what I think that movement means."

"And the rest?"

"I've got my own views. To me it was as though heaven was breaking through the veil, but I'd rather you questioned the acknowledged authorities."

What authorities? I thought. Were there any? Then I remembered that David had used the word "esoteric."

"David, you said that what makes great artists like Leonardo De Vinci, or Michelangelo, or Beethoven are questions really for the esoteric. What do you mean?

"Michael, this is not going to be easy."

David paused, wondering where he was going to begin.

"The word 'esoteric' denotes having a secret or hidden meaning or purpose; something that can only be understood by those who have received the necessary preparation or training. In physics or mathematics this is obvious, right?"

Michael nodded in agreement.

"Well, in the spiritual domain there is an implied training period for the candidate that culminates in a dramatic ritual. What is going to be expected of the candidate is enacted in an impressive, dramatic ritual that affects the person emotionally as well as intellectually; a personal initiation and potential entry into new knowledge that is hidden from those who are not ready or who have not been prepared. The ancients had this."

Michael nodded his understanding, remembering that he had heard from his Masonic father that drama and ritual are good teachers. But then he had to ask:

"You say you are now a practicing Christian. Is this true for Christianity too?"

"The New Testament tells us that Jesus passed on His Divine Knowledge directly to his twelve disciples. You'll remember that he had personally chosen them. He then prepared them to receive His new knowledge. Their job was to become stewards of 'the new mysteries,' and as such they were responsible to pass the new knowledge on to others whom they deemed able and ready to receive them; not to keep it to themselves as though it was theirs and theirs alone. We read that they did this faithfully, regularly healing the sick and driving out 'demons' or the 'complexes of the sub-conscious' in modern Jungian jargon. To those not ready or prepared, this divine knowledge was, of course, hidden, since they would have ridiculed it and spoiled it for the others."

We know this is all true because we read in the New Testament phrases like:

'It is given unto you to know the mysteries' and, 'we are the stewards of the mysteries of God'; 'having made known unto us the mysteries'; and 'we make known the mysteries of the gospels and the mystery which hath been hid from ages.'

"So what has happened in the last two thousand years then? Obviously something has gone wrong!" stated Michael as he peered at David. To Michael there was a clear disconnect between what David was saying and what went on in modern-day churches. Knowing David as he did, he wondered why he was still so enthusiastic as a Christian.

"What happened, Michael, is that this special knowledge that Jesus gave out to his closest disciples eventually became lost, and even to those high up in the church. Once Christianity became the official religion of the Roman Empire, more worldly knowledge, dogma, and state affairs slowly but surely pushed 'the mysteries' away into the background. So if you were a sincere seeker after Christ's highest teachings you would generally not find what you were looking for through church sermons and teachings."

"So is this then why other less visible spiritual groups sprang up to act as stewards of these teachings? If the churches couldn't or wouldn't act as stewards passing on this special knowledge, then other organizations would have to be set up to do the job, not so?"

"That's right, Michael."

"So this explains why they had to be secret too! It would have been a matter of life and death. I know my father believed that Freemasonry sprang from the network of Templars in the 1300's who had to go totally underground in England to escape the murder and torture that the Pope ordered inflicted on them, as had happened earlier in France on Friday the Thirteenth."

"You'll understand, Michael, then why the Freemasons in England only revealed themselves in 1717 when there was no more danger of the English church coming under the power of Rome."

"Yes, but what has this, David, to do with genius and the esoteric? Now is now. And then was then David. Times change, as you know."

"Just this, Michael. Times don't just change. They evolve in response to the forces and issues of the time. Many of the great men of science of the 1600's like Newton, Wren, and Boyle were Freemasons or members of less visible associated organizations that claimed to have this mystical knowledge. In many ways they have continued the teachings of The Essenes. Newton, for example, was a devoted Christian and applied his scholarship to religion and alchemy even more than he did to mathematics and physics. We now know that that it was

Freemasons who established The Royal Society with the new King's support. This ensured freedom of thought and the pre-eminence of the scientific method. Scientists in England were then able to meet freely together in public and publish their findings without fear of harassment or imprisonment. Before this, many would meet in secret and keep their discoveries to their own members. Some still do, of course."

Now, regarding music and this 'mystery symphony,' remember it was Newton who discovered the colors of the spectrum that blended together make white light. Newton reckoned that each musical note on the piano keyboard corresponded to a specific color, and that this correspondence operated in all the octaves of the piano and higher up too. In this regard he was following in the footsteps of Pythagoras and his followers."

"Go on David. This is fascinating."

What this means is that when we hear, say, the note D on the piano we should be able to see the color that is sympathetic to this note, if of course the internal light generated in sympathy in the brain is bright enough to be noticed by us, and if we are sufficiently sensitive."

"Well, that's amazing, David, because at my father's funeral when I asked my father how he was, I saw a picture of a bird—presumably a representation of his soul—leave his broken body and go up to heaven where you could hear Beethoven playing. But the music could be seen, too. The notes had their own individual colors."

"So, like some musicians, you Michael are one of those for whom music can also be seen. Some of my colleagues can tune their instruments by matching up the colors they see like a tuning fork. There are others who can hear what they see, but this is not as common. Was your father's funeral the first time for you?"

"Oh, no, this happened when I was very young. But I remember being told by my father that the colors weren't real, like my imaginary friends."

"Some folks, Michael, can taste music as well—sweet or sour or salty, etc. For others, each day of the week has its corresponding color. The world of our senses feeding into our mind from the brain is clearly more intertwined and connected than most of us think."

"So, wait a minute, David, are you saying that secret organizations with members such as Newton and the like are somehow connected with this lost truth that requires training and preparation? I don't see any evidence of this in my father, who was a Freemason as you know. And what has all this to do with Beethoven and this 'mystery symphony' with its message of impending disaster? Are you implying that Beethoven was a Freemason?"

"That's a good question, Michael. We know that Mozart, Haydn, Sibelius, and some other composers were Freemasons. Yet there is no solid evidence of Beethoven having been a member. One maxim that Beethoven kept framed on his desk written out in his own handwriting suggests a mystical influence and a personally meaningful one too:

'I am that which is, I am that that was, and that shall be. No mortal man hath lifted my veil. He is alone by Himself, and to Him alone do all things owe their being.'"

You see, to Beethoven, music was a link between the spiritual and the everyday life of the senses. He reveled in being alone in the countryside with nature. His own words above tell us that no mortal had lifted his veil. Rather, the Divine had done this, allowing him to see and hear God everywhere in nature. This he described in his pastoral symphony. Beethoven was a great enough man, Michael, that he did not need to have a near death experience to find attunement and communion with the divine! His own striving for the heavenly state brought this to him naturally!"

"I wish I had heard more about this from my father. That would have really interested me. Presumably then, there were known Freemasons in Beethoven's life, if this is true?"

David went again to the same bookcase and picked out another text from his library.

"We know that at least two men who influenced the young Beethoven greatly were prominent Freemasons. One was Neefe, a most cultured musician-composer and music teacher to the young Beethoven. The other was the witty, highly cultured, and linguistically talented Count Waldstein, whose friendship and early support of Beethoven in Bonn lasted most of the composer's life. Both saw the inner nobility in the young Beethoven which the composer felt keenly, lacking as he did the outer corresponding title and education that would have opened the doors to those who would have understood his music. But we must not forget the Countess Anna-Marie Erdödy and her husband Peter. The Countess was perhaps the most important of Beethoven's lady friends. Their close, albeit stormy, relationship helped him to survive the crisis of his oncoming deafness in the early 1800's. Her own health problems helped her to empathize with Beethoven. You can look forward to some good reading here David if you want to check her out."

Beethoven's favorable opinion of the British may also have been influenced by Count Waldstein, his great fans in London notwithstanding, of course. Desirous as he was to enter the British service, the Count raised an army in Germany in 1795 and then shipped it to England to support the fight against Napoleon. Later, in 1809, in fulfillment of these desires he served as a British colonel in the Austrian headquarters at the Battle of Aspern, which incidentally Napoleon lost, though he made up for this loss soon afterwards!"

"So, David, Beethoven had to fight to make his outer world conform to his inner nobility that he felt so keenly. And fight he certainly did, right?" asked Michael seeking reassurance that he was right, as though it really mattered to him. This made David think. Did Michael need to fight for his own inner nobility?

"Absolutely! In his spirit, Michael, Beethoven was like Napoleon. They were both imbued with an indomitable, heroic spirit, as was Newton, too. Each knew what he wanted and went after it in a most singular way, irrespective of what others said or did. And, by the way, it is said that Napoleon was Grand Master of one of the more secret Masonic organizations. He certainly protected the Masons after they were banned following the French Revolution. This may be one reason why Beethoven thought Napoleon should have acted better than he did when he crowned himself Emperor, and why he never spoke of him again after scratching out the dedication of his Eroica symphony to him."

"So, now David, are you telling me that Freemasonry spawns genius and divine revelation, and that I should have become a mason as my father wished?"

"No, I am not, Michael. I am giving you some historical facts to do with Beethoven as we know it. The question is: Are you thinking that? Perhaps you should have asked your father why he was a member and really listened to his answer instead of disregarding him as you obviously did. Remember, it's you who wants to understand this 'mystery symphony' and Beethoven's genius..."

JJ paused here in Michael's diary to reflect on him. His conflict with his father was truly palpable.

Michael's father wanted him to follow in his footsteps as a police officer and Freemason. Beethoven's father wanted his son to follow in Mozart's footsteps as a child prodigy. Since Beethoven's family was poor, this was understandable. Yet both their sons had their own ideas and strong wills, each becoming alienated from their fathers as a result.

JJ was reminded of Kahlil Gibran's writings on children—*they may come through us, but we don't own them or their thoughts. Their lives are their own to live.*

Beethoven certainly led his own life, thought JJ. He had to assert himself as a child just to survive his father's often brutal and drunken domination. So it is not surprising that he became intolerant of authority, and often showed contempt for the common opinions of others. JJ considered it for a moment. It was probably like this for Michael too.

He restarted Michael's audio journal.

After the usual conventions, Michael left David's house and went home to his flat in a most puzzled frame of mind. He wondered what it all meant and where it would lead. Looking back, he could say that, typical of youth, he had never had any difficulty in relegating some of his father's activities to the sidelines of life. Indeed, he had not even wondered if he had actually judged his father! He did wonder sometimes though if he had known his father at all! But then his father didn't know him either.

Michael rang me, explaining his difficulties, but assuring me of his best efforts although, for the moment, he confessed to being stumped in his investigation.

After listening attentively to his comments, I added to his confusion:

"It won't help you then, Michael, to know that Sir Henry still refuses to comment, refuses to play the symphony again for the present, and will not allow the score to be seen by others. Add that to your problem."

"Well, I'll be … What is this all about? How can a piece of music cause all this controversy? I am going to spend the next few hours listening to the ninth symphony, if I can stand it. Then I'm off to see Armstrong, the Principal of The Royal Academy of Music."

"Well, good luck to you, Michael," said JJ. He's gone all cagey and he tells me that Beynon is gravely ill with the doctor allowing no visitors and making no statement about his illness. By the way, I've sent a set of the symphonies and some piano works to your flat with a copy of Beethoven's life story. So you don't need to go out and buy anything or go to the library. "

Michael put the phone down, frowned, and scratched his head. Obviously there was something far beyond just the music. He suddenly realized it was the source of this music, the composer. There had been no conventional blurb in the papers. In fact, the whole thing was shrouded in mystery. Who was Beynon? How had an unknown harmony instructor persuaded Sir Henry to cancel an evening of Russian music to put on an unknown work? He had learned this by studying the program loaned to him by David Martin. There had been no program notes, merely the mention of a new symphony in four movements.

Michael opened my package and looked blankly at a pile of CDs and a huge book. Deciding that the book could wait, he put on the first movement of the ninth symphony and suffered solidly for twenty minutes or so. "Oh, well, try again. Did David say six times or twelve? Here goes."

Many hours later, Michael was surprised to find that the music started to have some meaning. He realized for the first time that music could say a great deal more than a book. His emotions were now disturbed, demanding understanding and resolution. As I listened to Michael's journal, it struck me that here Michael was teaching me. I adjusted my glasses several times. I didn't feel the emotions that Michael spoke about. Was I really a philistine?

Sleep that night was not easy for Michael's disturbed frame of mind. He decided that he had better interview

Armstrong at the Royal Academy of Music. After endless "hold on'-s" and "I sees" he finally got the Principal himself.

"Armstrong here."

"This is Lewis of *The Times* here. May I come and see you, Sir Herbert?"

"I'm rather busy," said Armstrong, "but what is the nature of your business, Mr. Lewis? You say you investigate matters for *The Times*. I assure you that life here is not complex; what do you wish to know from me?"

"My chief wants me to find out why so much mystery surrounds not only the symphony written by a chap named Beynon but about the man himself. I am told he is a teacher at the Royal Academy of Music and that he's ill. May I come and when, please?"

Michael seemed to wait interminably for an answer only to hear:

"I see."

"Sir Herbert, I assure you *The Times* is not after sensation. I can't escape the feeling there is something beyond just the identity of the composer. May I come please?"

"Very well, Mr. Lewis. Shall we say eleven o'clock tomorrow morning?"

Michael put the phone down. "Damn funny. Even he's reluctant to say anything."

As the inspector sat down and relaxed into his chair, he again had that sense of how his father would have enjoyed being at his side to meet Sir Herbert.

Michael spent the rest of the day listening to Beethoven's ninth symphony and reading extracts of his life story. He wondered over the twist of fate that resulted in Beethoven never having heard his greatest work played by an orchestra, and more extraordinary still, that he carried on composing in his new world of utter quiet and stillness. He could not understand how this was possible. Here was another mystery that was baffling about the man.

"Here am I now beginning to like the music that my father loved, and all because of the furor that this 'mystery symphony' (that I haven't heard yet) has aroused with its purported message of impending disaster. And if this isn't enough, the musicians are saying it could only have been written by Beethoven who has been dead for 180 years." Michael's tone of voice showed the depth of the challenge that was facing him.

Why do they dismiss the man Beynon who actually wrote it? Has some veil dropped over their eyes, deluding them? Or has this "mystery symphony" removed the veil as Beethoven wrote had happened to him?

The inspector recalled David's comments. Then it hit him.

"Good Lord, had Beethoven somehow been a steward of the mysteries?" He certainly had been true to himself as George Bernard Shaw had written. He got up and started to walk round his apartment with that characteristic gait of pursuing a crime to the very end.

"But if so, that would mean that Louis Beynon was also a 'steward of the mysteries' and that the "mystery symphony" was the result.

Challenge or no challenge, the inspector remembered his father's training. There must be an explanation and answer somewhere. He decided he had better find it. His job might just depend on it.

Resurrection's Instrument

Sir Herbert Armstrong sat in his office that morning with his oldest friend and colleague Arnold Paxton. They were both in their late fifties with graying hair and both looked like university dons. Each showed signs of distress and deeply felt grief. But it did not stop there. They were puzzled, too, as if neither could understand something. From time to time there would be a shake of the head, a pursing of the lips, a deep sigh. At last Armstrong said:

"I don't know what to make of it or what to tell this chap Lewis. Poor old Beynon has gone now and his last words make an even greater mystery of it all. If I tell this fellow what I really think, people will think I've gone mad. Yet I'm convinced it's the only explanation and that will prove to hoi polloi that I am crazy. What do you think? I want you to meet Lewis, too. You're the greatest authority on composition today and I want Lewis to hear your views."

Paxton grunted and nodded:

"Yes. When making an explanation, we'll likely be entering the realms of extra-sensory perception, the spirit world, and maybe heaven itself. There's only one way to handle this and that's to tell the facts as we know them and let Lewis interpret them for himself. Newspapers usually slant things or twist facts or tell half-truths or leave out facts to suit themselves. Let them shoulder the responsibility of interpreting themselves. Anyway, the letters they'll get if he even hints at our views at all will keep their letters to the editor going for years. Newspapers want increased circulation by hook or by crook, and I say let 'em earn it!"

"Right, I think our man has just arrived," said Armstrong as a knock sounded on the door. In answer to that, Armstrong's secretary announced:

"Mr. Lewis, Sir Herbert." Armstrong rose to meet him, shook hands, and introduced Paxton.

"Now, Mr. Lewis, you said on the phone that you are from *The Times*. What can I do for you?"

"Well, Sir Herbert, first of all, I'm no musician, and until last night, so-called 'classical music' left me unmoved. My chief has been astounded at the reactions all round to the first public performance of this chap Beynon's symphony. Our music critic Anthony Sargent, who is normally stinging in his comments, refuses to say a word. All enquiries to the conductor Sir Henry result in them getting their heads bitten off, and the orchestra is reluctant to play it again."

All Europe and now America wants the score, which Sir Henry won't release, and two ordinary music lovers seem to be worried about the interpretation of the work. Then there's the reaction of the orchestra and the audience on the night, plus this mysterious composer, and finally, I get the impression that there's something else I just can't put my finger on. Can you help?"

"Mr. Lewis, there's no mystery about Beynon as a man. I'm terribly upset to have to tell you that he died last night. He taught piano and harmony here for many years. Paxton and I were at his bedside. If you wish to unravel one little mystery here it is: Beynon kept saying to us, 'He keeps asking, have they understood? There's not much time left now.' We kept asking, 'Who's he?' only to be told the conductor."

"And you think this referred to the symphony?"

"It's only an opinion, because Beynon was semi-conscious and didn't recognize us; would you agree, Arnold?"

"Yes."

"Sir Herbert and you, Mr. Paxton, are internationally known authorities on music. Will you help? First of all, who was Beynon? What's his family history? Where did he come from?"

"Well, he sounded as English as you and me, but he once told me, laughingly, that his father had told him that the grandfather claimed the family hailed from a village just outside of Vienna."

"How did he come to the College?"

"He won a scholarship as a teenager in piano and did very well at harmony. He got the usual Academy awards and so on and was offered a teaching post, which he accepted, and there you are."

"Yes, but what of his activities here? Did no one here know that he was a composer? An unknown doesn't get someone like Sir Henry to put his one and only work on at Festival Hall. Surely, Sir Herbert, there's more to it than that?"

Armstrong looked at Paxton, sighed resignedly and said, "Very well, I am going back a few months and will try and relate events just as they occurred. I leave you to place your own interpretation on both them and the music.

"I refuse to be quoted in this respect and merely try and give you the gist of what Beynon told me and others from time to time.

"Louis Beynon sat down to breakfast that morning his mind in turmoil. Three times during the night he had woken up to the sound of a colossal orchestra rehearsing music quite unknown to him. Having been a musician all his life, he was puzzled at not being able to identify the work while immediately recognizing the significance of the composition. It was powerful, strong, disturbing. There was an immediacy about it."

Finishing his meal, he sat down at the piano and started to play the music that flooded his consciousness. In terms of the piano the music was insipid, and he realized at once that these sounds must be transferred in terms of the orchestra, and a great orchestra at that. Beynon had a good memory and, in a very short time, he had scored in a sketchy way a great deal of the opening movement. It would require constant revision and greater detail in the percussion section. He decided that he would concentrate on the tympani and effects portion of the orchestra at the afternoon rehearsal of the Royal College students' orchestra.

His concentrated study of the orchestral effects during the afternoon led him to his studio where he spent a few hours amending the score only to be interrupted by Armstrong's:

"Working late Louis?"

He hardly heard himself rudely retort, "Go away. I'm busy."

Armstrong, far from being outraged, asked, "What's that you were playing just now? It's great stuff, a new composition? Yours?"

The answer staggered Armstrong.

"I don't know frankly. This has been pounding away in my head for hours, not a tune but a full orchestra and I'm scoring it. Is there such a thing as extra-sensory perception in this field?"

"I see what you mean. Tunes can pass quite easily between people but this, I don't know. How did it start?"

"Three times during last night I was woken up with this pounding away inside me. It was as if a symphony orchestra was trying to break out."

Armstrong thought for a moment. "It's nothing I know or can recall from what I heard, but it's redolent of—" he gazed fixedly at Beynon. "It's occurred to you, I'm sure."

Beynon stared back. "Yes," he replied, "but it's quite impossible; you know every major work of Beethoven's, as I do."

"Well, good night."

Beynon sat quite still for a long time after Armstrong had gone and repeatedly murmured to himself, "So he thinks so, too. God, what is happening to me?"

Feeling that a long walk in the cool of the evening was called for, he started walking over the fields of Regent's Park only to feel an irresistible force that directed him to his flat in St. John's Wood.

Surrendering to this hidden urge, he arrived home and, after eating his supper slowly and unenthusiastically, retired early to bed. It seemed to him that sleep was not long in coming, but once again he was wide awake staring at his alarm clock showing 4:00 a.m. Once more he had not slept. The mighty orchestra had been pounding out its message, this time an obvious, slow movement. Slow, yes, but so beautiful, so divine, so tragic, so urgent, and yet expressing endless time. Four glorious soprano voices had introduced the second theme of the movement and he rushed to his piano to score the parts still fresh and strong in his mind.

Like Beethoven before him, he had been playing and occasionally singing for over an hour during the night when his landlady opened the door exclaiming, "Mr. Beynon, really! It's the middle of the night! Must you wake everybody up? I've been listening to you for ages and I've never heard anything like it. It's so beautiful and yet so sad and tragic, what is it?"

Beynon looked blankly at her and said, "Mrs. Todd, he says it's a Requiem mass for mankind."

"Who says? You're composing, aren't you?"

"Me?" said Beynon, "I'm only recording it. I wish I could compose like that. He says it's the Tenth and I must hurry up as there's little time for me and not much for the world."

"Are you all right, Mr. Beynon?" asked Mrs. Todd, "You seem strange."

"Please go back to bed. It's gone now."

"What's gone?"

"The orchestra, the music. I can go to sleep now."

Beynon returned to his room, only to be back at the piano at seven o'clock once more playing some parts again; but now a new development had come about, as the piano was put to its limits, causing everything in the room to rattle. Mrs. Todd's reproaches were ignored as Beynon finally collapsed over his instrument from sheer exhaustion. A frantic call was placed to Dr. Jacobs, who arrived and diagnosed the trouble as mental and physical exhaustion. Dr. Jacobs returned to Mrs. Todd's lounge to question her but could make little sense of her comments.

"Tell me, Mrs. Todd, he keeps mumbling something about 'he must get it down in music' and then he made me jump saying, 'All right, Ludwig, give me time, I'm working as quickly as I can. You must play the scherzo and last movement again. *No*, no, no, speak English, my German is not good enough.' He's hysterical and I've given him a strong sedative which should put him to sleep for hours."

Mrs. Todd frowned and said, "I don't know, doctor; when I suggested he was composing, he denied it and said he was only recording it and wished he could compose like that. Then he seemed to wake up and go back to bed."

"Call me again then if he has any more of these turns won't you?"

"Very well doctor ... "

Armstrong paused after this long dissertation and turned to Paxton saying, "I think you had better carry on from there, Arnold. I could, of course, but you must remember some of what you told me at the time."

"Very well, Herbert, I'll try as best as I can."

"It was about a month ago ... Paxton returned home one evening a very puzzled man. All his life he had hoped that one day he would find amongst his students that one person who might possess the divine spark, that one brain which could produce something new, something original, moving, upsetting; someone whose music was not of the general run of things. In his kindly way he hoped that he might be of help to a young genius, say another Delius or Debussy."

Today had not only shocked him, but shattered him. He had been passing a studio along his passage and was struck by the music emanating from Beynon's room. Believing at first that it was a student, he was about to move on, but was halted by the curious and sudden change of moods in the music. He stopped to listen and was thrilled to realize that here at last was the realization of a lifelong ambition. This was not only an original composition, but strong, forceful stuff the like of which belonged only to perhaps one man in a generation. Deciding not to interrupt, he very quietly slipped through the door and sat down. Beynon had not heard him, thank heavens. He was playing the coda of a slow movement of almost unbearable beauty yet tragic and suddenly had leapt into a scherzo which he could only interpret as someone making a desperate plea which was brutally but emphatically rejected. Paxton sat entranced for nearly an hour as Beynon worked, obviously recording from memory and not composing at all."

At times he would be speaking to himself as if trying to convince himself of the accuracy of his memory. The words dropped were at first meaningless, until Paxton suddenly realized not only were they very pointed, but illuminating, once the connection was understood. "So Franz thought I had written everything, he admits he was wrong... Richard says this should be named 'Götterdämmerung'... Now Johann Sebastian says he's got to write another passion because God has condemned all religion and religious men."

So it went on until a final remark made Paxton gasp. "And where on earth will they get the first violins to match Paganini, Joachim, Ysaye, Fritz and the others?" Beynon stopped abruptly on hearing Paxton and remarked quite casually, "Oh, hello, there you are. You surprised me."

"Well, you didn't surprise me, you shocked me, and I might say you mesmerized me. What on earth is that music?" Beynon looked at Paxton, but his mind was far away.

"On earth did you say? It's certainly not that, I assure you."

"Those remarks you made just now. What do they mean—those great violinists of the past?"

"Oh, them. Yes, they were there. You've never heard such beautiful strings; the playing was just beyond description or criticism. He must have his hearing back to normal because he embraced them one by one and said he bent his knee to them."

"He?" said Paxton. "Who's he?"

Beynon looked blankly at Paxton and said, "What are you talking about? Good-night!" and gathered up his papers and passed out into the passage.

Paxton looked at his listeners and continued, "That was the beginning of quite a long, you might say 'musical association' because from then on he would often ask me if certain passages could be right. He would accept no criticism of counterpoint or harmony, merely retorting 'There are no laws for him, he makes them and breaks them.'"

I could never get any explanation of anything. I was only conscious that something of gigantic importance was being constructed before my very eyes. Every phrase, every development was shrieking Beethoven at me and I could say nothing."

The inspector stirred uneasily and asked, "You never, as it were, tried to force an answer out of him?"

"Only once, and he looked at me and said 'This will explain itself given time. I mean, if I am given time.'"

Paxton continued, "The climax, in a sense, came one afternoon when he asked if I thought the Principal, Sir Herbert here, would permit him to rehearse the first movement of a work he'd scored for the orchestra. Until then, he'd never done any conducting but I took it upon myself to say yes. Sir Herbert agreed at once and it was only then that we discussed our own experiences with Beynon. Here I must confess we never got anywhere. Hard as we tried he would never give us any direct answers."

Paxton went on, "From the first rehearsals with the orchestra playing from manuscript there was trouble. Beynon was no trained conductor, but he knew what he wanted and used no tact. He bawled at his players and, on more than one occasion, he snarled 'Thank God he didn't hear that.' Curiously enough, this very young orchestra slowly became engrossed and even over-awed not by Beynon, but by the music itself, and young McCallum the leader confessed to me that this music, the first movement, was frightening him. He said it was as if each time they rehearsed it was reiterating some warning of a catastrophe to come."

The inspector, who had been looking more and more puzzled, finally blurted out, "But what is this all about? It's just beyond me!"

"Beyond you," said Paxton, "it's beyond anyone and yet the force of it is almost paralyzing. However, I'll continue."

During one rehearsal Sir Henry was present when Beynon was calling the first violins a lot of imbeciles. "Have you no fear of death" he asked them? If so, please show it!"

Sir Henry, who had been listening completely absorbed for some time, felt this was uncalled for and interjected 'Really, Louis, that's ridiculous!' He was told curtly, 'Be quiet—when I want opinions I'll ask for them, but as far as this work goes I need none. He made it absolutely clear.' Sir Henry, of course, asked who 'he' was, and Beynon retorted, 'There's only one he; now be silent and don't interrupt.' He was quite rude, really, but Sir Henry was utterly enraptured and sat through the third rehearsal of the complete movement. Nothing would satisfy Beynon. At times he would stop the orchestra for nearly a minute while it seemed he might be recalling or listening to something and off they would go again. At last he said 'All right, that will do. But I must get the Royal Philharmonic,' and with that he collected the scores and went straight home, refusing to speak to anyone."

Paxton paused before going on, "Please be patient, this takes a lot of explaining. During the next fortnight he seemed quite frantic when he again asked for the orchestra. He now had completed the slow movement. Don't ask me about the sopranos, and the scherzo. This was all leading up to a colossal last movement and we were all very curious to know how the work would come to an end."

"What happened then?" asked the inspector.

"It was near the end of term and Beynon, without a word to a soul, went to visit some monastery in Crete. We only learned this later."

"You mean the Greek island of Crete in the Mediterranean?"

"Yes, we cannot be sure, but my guess is that it was to do with this mystery symphony."

"What makes you think that?" asked Lewis.

"Well," said Paxton, "we found in Beynon's studio a book on spirituality by a Greek scholar, as well as one to do with retracing the footsteps of two 6th century Syrian monks by an Oxford scholar. You're the investigator, you tell me. However, that wasn't all we heard. Sir Herbert will tell you he received calls from the Greek Orthodox Church, as well as some from those engaged in research into extra-sensory perception. To cut the thing short, some of them thought Beynon to be quite eccentric because of the questions he asked. There is, however, one story which can be given at firsthand because one of our professors of

BEETHOVEN'S TENTH SYMPHONY

the violin is interested in this spiritualist stuff. I've asked her to be within call so that she can relate what happened. Would you like to hear it, Mr. Lewis?"

"Yes, absolutely, Professor Paxton," said Lewis enthusiastically.

Paxton pressed the bell and to the secretary said, "Please ask Ms. Billson if she would come in now." A few minutes later Ms. Billson, a pleasant woman of some forty odd years, took her seat after being introduced to Lewis.

"Miss Billson," said Armstrong, "will you please tell Mr. Lewis exactly what happened the time you attended a session at Madame Sabine's place?"

"Well, Sir Herbert, as you know I go now and again and this time I was quite surprised to see Louis Beynon in the waiting room. He didn't even greet me. He was miles away, as if in another world. He just gazed into space, sitting motionless. Eventually, Madame, her real name is Edwards, came in and we all sat round the table. Madame's practice was to go off into a sort of trance and then address all with a message for one of us. This night was quite different. I speak fairly good German but Madame does not do so at all. You can imagine my astonishment when she started off 'He says tell Louis …' Then in German as if repeating verbatim, 'Go home at once and get on with the last movement, don't waste time, you have so little left.' Beynon sat up straight, as if shocked, and quickly left the room. Madame came round and said curtly that that was all for the evening. Later, when I asked her about it she said vaguely, 'I've seen paintings of him somewhere, he was an elderly man, rather swarthy but very pressing.' I didn't understand at all and still don't. Can you say?"

Inspector Lewis stirred restively and asked Miss Billson, "Can you make no explanation of this incident?"

"Only one I can't accept myself. It's too fantastic to even mention seriously," replied Miss Billson.

"You mean—?"

"I mean Madame was in contact with Beethoven. Now laugh, I can't. I am too puzzled by the whole thing. Goodbye." Miss Billson left the room and there was silence for a long time.

Finally, the inspector said "Well, gentlemen, what do you make of that?"

Sir Herbert looked at Paxton who remarked, "You do the making, Mr. Lewis; form your own conclusions. We're musicians—not magicians, nor spiritualists. I say one thing only. When I watched Beynon he was not composing, he was recording on paper the music in his head. He orchestrated at once and I remind you he was a pianist and has, until now, never written anything for instruments, and to begin on a colossal symphony like this is beyond my understanding."

The inspector stared for a long time at the musicians and finally declared, "Very well, Sir Herbert, the composition's origin we'll leave for the time being, but will you assist me in this aspect of the work. From the discussions I've had with many people, both professionals like yourselves and just plain music lovers, I'm forced to the opinion that there's more to it than that. One man has said that it's an indictment of man, another has said it's a message from another world, a third has said it's a warning. I'm told your own young orchestra here was frightened by it and that Beynon had a lot of trouble getting them to repeat the first movement until he was satisfied. Musicians tell me the trouble was not technical but the reaction within the players. One or two started to shiver. Now what on earth can cause that?"

Armstrong muttered, "On earth did you say?"

Paxton echoed him, "ON EARTH is the question and damned if I can answer it!"

The inspector, showing his determination, resumed the attack. "Please gentlemen, you mention a message or someone does. Help me to understand so that I can help others. I make no comment about an after-life and all the theories and beliefs about heaven and hell and so on. What do you read into this astonishing music?"

"Well, Mr. Lewis," said Armstrong, "Since you put it like that, let me say that I'm no romantic and always avoid the popular interpretations and romantic nonsense written about great music. Most of it is commercial advertising put out by the publishers for consumption by the general public who will swallow mostly anything they read. I'll give you my views, but I want your word not to quote my name or Paxton's."

"You have my word, Sir Herbert," stated Lewis.

"Thank you. By now you will have gathered that there certainly is a mystery surrounding this composition. Beynon's own comments show that he never actually composed this music. That aspect I leave you to explain, if you can. I shall merely try to give my interpretation of the message and warning that the first movement conveys to me and Arnold here. Possibly Beynon's own remarks have directed our thoughts."

"I have no idea Sir Herbert what you mean when you say that Beynon's own comments show that he did not compose the music. But please, go on."

"Well, the movement opens very brightly, in a way reminiscent of the joy expressed in Beethoven's ninth. There's the grandeur and majesty of his gates of heaven, as it were. Then hesitation and doubt creep into this conception. I get the feeling of a celestial jury reviewing the world or mankind. I hear arguments for and against. There's pleading, then terrible condemnation, and finally impatience with the whole matter as if the judge had ruled the whole case not worth the bother of summing up. The jury is summarily dismissed and God sentences man not only to eternal damnation but total destruction.

"How can that be Sir Herbert" asked the inspector, sounding totally bewildered.

"He feels that man's wickedness, always perpetrated in His name, can only be punished by dissolution. The indictment is total. At first I thought this was going to be self-destruction by man but it goes beyond that, and I now feel that it will be by some extraterrestrial action, say something like a giant meteor colliding with Earth, a sort of Exodus, but in this case the whole earth, and destroying every living thing in it. The fury is certainly excruciating and agonizing. The world is to become a gigantic necropolis and this you can perceive in the slow movement which follows."

Michael started to fidget as though trying to come to grips with this dreadful prognosis.

"Good heavens, Sir Herbert, are you serious? What proof can there be of the existence of this threat? I can't possibly print that. Some folks would go mad."

Armstrong retorted, "Some folks would say that you were talking utter rubbish."

The inspector pondered deeply for a long time and finally said, "But, really, I don't know what to say gentlemen, it's fantastic. You assure me that with all your knowledge of music that Beynon did not compose this music?"

"That is so, Mr. Lewis. We are quite certain of that and, of course, Beynon's own comments from time to time are an admission to that effect."

"I want to thank you, Sir Herbert, and you Mr. Paxton, for your kindness and time. I must confess I'm staggered and quite out of my depth: firstly the origin of the music and secondly the warning from God knows where?"

"Exactly the right words, Mr. Lewis. We wish you good morning and I hardly need add that we look forward with keen anticipation to the results of your investigation."

"Good day gentlemen, and once again, thank you," replied the inspector, hoping himself that there would indeed be results forthcoming that would satisfy his boss.

The inspector left the Royal Academy of Music a sorely puzzled man, wondering if he was going a little 'off his rocker.' Try as he might by dismissing all that stuff about warnings and messages, the facts surrounding the composition were undeniable and, in his mind, inexplicable. Lewis was no believer in reincarnation, nor was he impressed with spiritualism, particularly since a Jesuit Father had once told him that as man had never learned anything from the so-called spirits that he didn't already know, there was no reason to believe in their existence or take the theory seriously.

That was all very well, but if Beynon did not write the symphony, who did? If reincarnation was the answer why then was he, up until now, just another musician of no particular attainment? There was no evidence, until now, that Beynon was even worthy of the title "composer." The masterpieces of Bach, Mozart, Beethoven, Brahms, or Chopin did not appear with a bang. They evolved from earlier works and were the results of a lifetime of experience.

I listened to more of Michael's comments in his diary: "... Here was a man who writes one work, a colossal work, and dies. The work is not only attributed to a genius of years ago, but carries a crazy warning if one is to believe these interpretations ..."

Michael felt so muddled up he decided to get drunk after he'd completed his notes.

"Oh, let the notes wait; a good stiff drink's the answer, or two, or three. Maybe I'll wake up sizzled and in the right mood to start thinking afresh." He retired to bed quite late. But he was to know no peace.

♪

JJ decided that his news could not wait and called Michael late at night.

"Well, Michael, how are you getting on? I've got some news for you."

"Hello, JJ, I've got some for you. I know I'm tight but if what I've heard is true then not only Beethoven is alive but also all the old masters and musicians playing up hell in heaven. That can't be right, can it?"

"Michael you drunken clot, sober up. What's come over you? There's a lot at stake here for *The Times*."

"Awful dream, JJ. Dreamt the world was coming to an end and as the last bowler hat floated down the Thames, someone said 'Thank God it's by a reputable maker.' Was it H.G. Wells who said that?"

"Go and dip your head in cold water and ring me back in half an hour, I want you sober in my office at eleven this morning. There've been some developments and old Malcolm won't say a word about his inviting some of the world's greatest musicians to a mini-conference. Come on, sober up. Things are happening."

Was the world going to come to an end? Michael did not know, but found it unbelievable to think that it would be announced in this way, a symphony no less, and then one which the musicians said had to be from Beethoven who was long dead. But then if people could make it to heaven, perhaps it was no more out of the ordinary than angelic announcements in the Bible.

♪

Michael rose that morning in no better frame of mind. He could not accept the origins of the symphony, neither could he credit Beynon with its composition. What was the answer? As for the warning about the end of the world, that too he was loath to take seriously. Ever since he could remember, there had been some cranky so-called prophet prophesying destruction only to be proved to be off the wall subsequently. On the other hand, the established religions keep plugging the coming of the Messiah and a judgment day. As far as he could see, no one really took this seriously and no church dignitary seemed in any hurry to go to heaven.

Yet, there was still the existence of this "mystery symphony" to be explained away. Michael came to the conclusion that he had better stop thinking about it or he would once more seek the assistance of the bottle. He knew he couldn't blow this since I was counting on him.

He walked into my office surprised at the presence of Anthony Sargent, the *Times* music critic, who hardly seemed to notice him coming in.

"Hello, JJ, hello Anthony, you here too?"

"Hello, Michael, what's come over you? Why the celebration last night?"

"Celebration be damned. I wasn't celebrating. I was commiserating with myself. I've never come across anything like this before and I haven't the faintest idea of what the heck is going on. Either I have to ridicule the suggestion that dead men write music, which professional musicians are set on, or I've got to invite my readers to have me put in a mental hospital by saying that they do. That's the problem I tried to solve in the pub last night. If I predicted the destruction of the world as the message implies in this music you would have me writing daily zodiac stuff instead of Lilly Smith, our tame astrologer."

"Most interesting," said Sargent, "really interesting."

"I knew it. I knew it. I knew there was something going on from the start of that musical business. Now then, Michael, tell me from the beginning what you have found out. You be quiet Anthony, don't interrupt," JJ interjected abruptly.

"Right," said the inspector. "Listen carefully and believe me, I am not exaggerating. Having a good memory, I'll try to give it to you verbatim."

For the next hour the inspector related very slowly and impressively the results of his interviews, finishing with Armstrong and Paxton but withholding their names. Through it all Sargent had nodded his head emphatically and obviously wanted to interject with his comments.

JJ had not said a word when he went to his glass cabinet to return with a bottle of whiskey and three glasses. He filled them generously and passed them around.

"I see why you tried to solve your problems in the pub," announced JJ. "Good Lord! Are we to accept that and publish it? That Beynon gets a symphony from Beethoven in heaven presumably and it contains a warning that fairly soon the world is to be destroyed by God bringing about some celestial action to punish mankind? And then he dies himself!"

There was silence, until JJ spoke:

"Why celestial, would that mean extraterrestrial, space stuff?"

To which Sargent now replied, "A good guess, JJ. Do you remember the legend of Prometheus? He was chained to a mountain rock for bringing fire to mankind. This was supposed to be in the time of Moses. Oh, yes, this is relevant. The theme used in Beethoven's overture, Prometheus, can be heard quite clearly and incisively on the horns under the rolling of the tympani in the first movement. Your informant was most discerning Michael.

"So that's where he got it from, I see. But, JJ, you said you had some news?"

Drumming my fingers on the table for a moment I replied, "I have heard from my contacts that Sir Henry is organizing a sort of meeting of leading conductors, scientists, and church folk to discuss this work. It's clear he knows what you've told us, Michael, and it's equally obvious he's put a similar interpretation on it. My contacts tell me that the conference will be held at some academy in Crete. We know that Beynon went to visit a monastery on the island of Crete, but why this conference will be held there, I don't know. I'm going to try to be at this gathering and, if Sir Henry will allow it, I want you, Michael, to come with me. I don't want your investigation to stall. I am trusting this will give us the leads we need. This won't be a holiday for you, Michael. When Sir Henry knows that we know, he'll just have to let us attend. We shall have to be most discreet in reporting this to the public."

I had chosen my words carefully, but Michael knew we needed answers. His frustration erupted, "Traditionally, it's the doom and gloom religious folk telling us to repent since the end of the world is nigh because we are all sinners, and of course without any evidence! And we are still here. Then on the other side we have the modern environmentalists acting like religious fanatics insisting that there is irrefutable scientific evidence that modern greenhouse gases are the entire cause. Non-believers are pilloried, even questioning scientists. Yet we're told there have been ice ages before and the earth's magnetic field has flipped several times without our help. Now there's this "mystery symphony" announcing the same thing and which the musicians are saying could only have been written by a dead Beethoven, and that the expected destruction will now come through an extraterrestrial event. What does that mean? Comets, meteors, cosmic rays?"

No one said anything.

♪

At the other end of town, Sir Henry needed to ground himself. He decided to get a scientific opinion from a famous scientist with whom he had shared digs when a student. He was hoping it would dispel his fears for the future.

A Scientific Opinion

Dr. R.W.B Stevens, Professor of Physics at Imperial College and a renowned scientist and author, was a very puzzled man—not because of anything connected with his research into the universe and black holes. Roger was amazed because a famous conductor had just requested him to listen carefully to some new piece of music.

"Can this be for real? This must be a hoax."

That morning on looking in his in-tray he saw that he had received by courier a parcel with a letter inside from Sir Henry Malcolm. The two of them had shared digs together as students when Henry had been a student at The Royal Academy of Music and he a student in the Physics department at Imperial College. He read the letter:

Roger, the recording enclosed is of a new symphony about which there is a definite mystery. Please listen to it at least three or more times, pay very close attention, and then, I trust you will be kind enough to receive myself and my wife Lady Audrey at your college apartment on Queen's Gate for a discussion which may well be somewhat long in duration. Please take this request most seriously. I think you will be intrigued by the music. You are about the only person I can turn to in this regard.

Roger was so intrigued he started thinking out loud. "But Henry, you are the musician. I am a mathematician and scientist. Why are you asking me? I am no musician. Do you mean my wife Sarah? Yes, I certainly enjoy Beethoven and Mozart, but I also like The Beatles, and the bagpipe bands on the march."

Roger's wife Sarah was a cellist, so he knew she would want to hear this piece of music. That evening at their home he set up the music equipment and joined her to listen. He was a little surprised when at the end of the first movement she shouted, "Roger, stop there, now go back and play that again!" He did so, only to be told: "Now again, right from the beginning to the end." It had not ended there because she had not been satisfied until the whole symphony had been played yet again. Finally, she said in a very quiet voice,

"I see. Yes, Sir Henry is right, Roger. There's something most strange about this."

"What do you make of it then, darling?" said Roger, noting the strangeness and trepidation in her voice.

Sarah didn't really want to talk. She did not like the emotions that this piece of music generated in her. It sent shivers up and down her spine. It was threatening, she told Roger, and yet it seemed to beckon to the future. Some parts reminded her of Beethoven though she couldn't identify the piece.

The doorbell rang.

Sir Henry and Lady Audrey arrived as expected and were greeted by Sarah and Roger Stevens. They both looked in their late fifties or early sixties. Sir Henry was tall and imposing with a long, expressive face. He looked the typical part of a great musician and conductor. He was well-groomed yet with long, light brown graying hair that could suddenly fall out of place over his head and face. Lady Audrey was somewhat petite and quite beautiful, with a peaches and cream complexion that would have made her stand out in London society if she had wanted this. She was the practical brains behind her husband and was most comfortable in her role. She knew that her husband would really excel as a conductor if he could focus entirely on his music, and not worry about the details of daily living. Despite being an accomplished pianist in her own right, Lady Audrey decided to give Sir Henry the opportunity to surpass himself and be in the background herself. Sir Henry knew he was a lucky man. He got down to business straightaway.

"Did you or your wife listen to it Roger, and would you care to make any comment? I don't wish to prompt you in any way and I'll explain why in a few moments."

"Well, Henry, I can't comment as a musical critic like Sargent does in *The Times*, but my wife certainly can, being a cellist. Tell Sir Henry, darling, what you experienced."

Sarah composed herself and looked straight at Sir Henry. She was a little nervous at being face to face with such a world-renowned conductor. "There's surely some sort of warning of a horrible catastrophe, Sir Henry. It made me feel quite uncomfortable. I'm no expert but can this be modern music? Roger and I couldn't escape the feeling that it was the work of one of the old great masters; Beethoven, I would say."

Sir Henry looked at Sarah and then at his old roommate and said, "I can tell you this. It's not one of these so-called works discovered in an attic and that sort of nonsense. I want to tell you now the origin of this music and how I came to be associated with it. It's a very long story and I'll have to refer to my notes. I ask you to be patient with me because at the end I will be asking you some questions. Roger you are one of the very few scientists that I feel can give me some answers here.

"Very well, Henry. Take your time. I feel sure this is not just a musical quiz."

"Far from it, Roger, although of course it is the sudden appearance of this symphony under the most extraordinary circumstances which needs explaining in the first place, and in the second, whether the interpretation put on it by some famous musicians can and should be taken seriously."

"I see," said Roger.

Very slowly and impressively Sir Henry told the story, beginning with his first hearing of the rehearsal at The Royal Academy of Music, subsequent rehearsals, Paxton's experiences, then the first public performance at Festival Hall. Before touching on his own upcoming conference, he covered in great detail all the other incidents which, taken together, presented a seemingly insoluble problem.

"All along, I had felt the force of this work and during the first real performance I somehow felt that I was not conducting it myself but some inner force was guiding me as this part was stressed or that broadened and so on. In fact, the interpretation of the work as a whole was not my own and I noticed that Lunn, the leader of the orchestra, was quite surprised when certain passages were conducted and directed in a manner quite different from the rehearsal. Beethoven was very generous in his markings on his scores and it was as if my score was not definite enough and needed re-editing. The net result of all of this was that I left the concert hall abruptly, too disturbed to conform to conventions, and went home. Audrey usually recorded my broadcasts and by good fortune she had done so this time. I decided that after you and I had met, as we are today, that I would call together some of the leading musicians in the world and people connected with psychic research, extra sensory perception, reincarnation, the churches, etc. I am hoping that someone, somehow, will remove from my mind the horrible forebodings that are with me now. You see, the bits of music that Sarah recognized were of course from Prometheus and the main motif of the fifth symphony."

Since it seemed that some extraterrestrial action was the likely means for bringing about the destruction of life in our world, I thought of you of course and decided to send you the recording of the symphony and see how you reacted to it. But first I wanted to do some reading of my own before seeing you in person. I know it's popular science and quite dated now, but I started by reading Velikovsky's 'Worlds in Collision' that you loaned me when we shared digs together. I wondered if Venus, supposedly once a comet and which might have caused the Exodus in the Bible by coming very close to Earth, could somehow do it again. But Venus is a planet and to me this just didn't seem possible."

Professor Stephens nodded his agreement to this.

"Surely you didn't stop there, Henry?"

Sir Henry paused as he seemed to be marshalling his thoughts.

"No, but I am so very diffident about babbling on about subjects so beyond my understanding. I had reached the stage when I was convinced that there were other possibilities. I started to read anything that had a possible bearing on my obsession. You had been interested in Carl Sagan as a student so I got a copy of his Cosmos TV series and watched that."

"I found it most interesting. I heard Dr. Sagan say that comets were like giant snowballs, which seemed odd. He mentioned the Tunguska explosion in 1908 in Russia and said this had been caused by debris from a passing comet. I later read that this explosion and fireball in the sky over an uninhabited part of Siberia was 1000 times more powerful than the atomic bomb that destroyed Hiroshima and that it flattened 800 hundred square miles of forest. That taught me that extraterrestrial threats are real, and that comets can be lethal. What's your take on this Roger?"

"Well, if that Tunguska explosion, Henry, had happened over a modern big city like London when you and

I were students, not only would the two of us not be here, but an additional 300,000 Londoners would have been killed by the explosion and all buildings flattened in a twelve mile radius of the center."

"My God, Roger. That's really frightening! Could this happen again?"

"Well, they have certainly happened in the past Henry, but the truth is that these sorts of collisions and near collisions are happening all the time. Five hundred years ago a meteor shower killed 10,000 in China. This is not surprising since we now know that about 4,000 asteroids half a mile or so in diameter cross Earth's orbit every year. Any one of them could wipe out our world if they hit us."

"So is it then, Roger, just a question of time before one hits us again?"

"Well, you could say that, but it's actually not as simple as that, Roger, since the earth's surface is mostly water. It depends where they hit, too. We now know that there can be great collisions in our solar system."

Sir Henry had recently read that many scientists did not really believe in the possibility of these large cosmic collisions hitting Earth until they actually saw a comet in 1994 smack into Jupiter with a force equivalent to 40 million megatons of TNT. The scientists had added that if that comet had hit the Earth every living thing on the planet would have been wiped out. These scientific facts added to Sir Henry's worried frame of mind.

"My God, Roger, this is certainly not public knowledge."

"That's true, Henry. But then the public does not know either that just over the last 500 million years there have been about five major extinctions of various living species on our planet. You've heard Roger about how the dinosaurs died out, haven't you?"

Sir Henry knew that 65 million years the dinosaurs had died out and that this was likely due to a comet hitting the earth or through repeated asteroid collisions. But he did not know that associated with the solar system moving through the Milky Way there's also a 62 million year cycle where excessive cosmic radiation itself periodically kills off a lot of species, including marine life.

"But the next one is far away Henry," added Roger. Roger noticed that Sir Henry was noticeably agitated, thumbing his fingers on the table quite loudly.

"So Henry, we don't have to worry about that!"

But Sir Henry's worried demeanor didn't change.

"Life on earth, Roger, is clearly a lot more precarious than we have been led to believe. There seem to be built-in cycles and mechanisms for periodically destroying life on earth. Didn't Einstein say that God does not play dice with the universe? I guess he didn't know about these mass extinctions going back millions of years. It looks like he got it wrong!"

"But Henry, you have only seen one side of it. Life and the universe run on cycles. Periodic cycles of destruction in Earth's history also mean periodic cycles for new beginnings that allow new species and life forms to form and flourish such as the dinosaurs. Another cycle of destruction then removed them so that new species could flourish."

Professor Stephens saw that this was not registering with Sir Henry who was away somewhere with his thoughts.

"Well, if everyone's reaction to this 'mystery symphony' is like mine, Roger, then there's another cosmic collision in the works right now. The question is, can you see anything special on the horizon that speaks to this warning?"

Professor Stephens ruminated on what to say. Sir Henry waited with his own baited breath.

"I can't be sure here, Henry. But I can tell you that there was likely one quite recently, around 1200 B.C, in all likelihood linked to the end of the Bronze Age. We know that around that time the climate all over the Earth changed suddenly and got a lot colder, lasting nearly 400 years."

"Well, in about 86 to 100 years time the same conditions will arise again. The chances are once more fifty-fifty for a major collision. There is also a possibility of a major collision much sooner—around 2012—although much less than fifty-fifty. It is certainly not fashionable these days to mention this, but Newton came up with several dates for the end times from studying the Bible. 2060 was one of his dates."

"Oh my God, that's it," said Sir Henry with trepidation and song in his voice, "that's the meaning of the warning! I knew it. I knew it. What shall I do, Roger?"

"There's nothing you can do, Henry. It may happen. It may not happen. Is there any point in telling people this? Many would die of fright. You've heard about when the Americans broadcast H.G. Well's 'War of the Worlds,' haven't you?"

"Yes, of course. How long before all life is extinct once destruction begins and what will be the first indication that the holocaust has begun?"

Roger thought for a moment. "I can only give you a rough estimate for a major collision. I would say one to two weeks would be sufficient to destroy nearly everything living. But Henry, my calculations are preliminary."

Sir Henry then asked the obvious, "With our current scientific understanding and increasing space technology is there anything that you can envisage that our scientists, and especially the Americans, could do to avert this catastrophe? After all, if this eventually gets out to the general public and not just to governments, there will be terrific pressure on governments to develop some means of averting this disaster; even if there is only a miniscule chance of success. That's of course assuming that people don't panic leading to its own destruction."

Roger looked upwards to think for a moment. "Well, the U.S 'Stars Wars' program could be used to detonate a nuclear device right ahead of these comets or asteroids. I think NASA has already a plan in place here. But the force of such a nuclear explosion will likely not be enough to avert the calamity."

Sir Henry paused to think for a moment and then abruptly got up to leave with Lady Audrey, who had just entered the room with Sarah Stephens.

"Please keep me informed, Henry, and my comments confidential."

Sir Henry nodded .

Sir Henry and Lady Audrey bade farewell to Roger and Sarah after thanking them, and returned to their home in preparation for their upcoming conference in Crete. They couldn't help wondering what they were going to tell this group of famous conductors, clergy, and ESP scientists—"Darling, can we actually say that there is a very real physical basis in the future for the warning in the mystery symphony that the world is to be destroyed? Will anybody believe us not knowing who was saying this? Would this lead to panic around the world considering the reaction so far to this 'mystery symphony'?"

Sir Henry stared blankly at his wife Audrey, frowned, muttered, and finally blurted out: "What the devil am I to tell them, my dear? Shortly we'll have many of the greatest conductors in the world together in Crete as well as these intellectual chaps who'll probably laugh their heads off. I just don't know how to start."

Lady Audrey gazed tenderly at her husband and smiled. Except when playing or conducting he was really a big over-grown child. Quite impractical in worldly affairs, too credulous by half, he was the target for anybody with a hard-luck story or a willing victim for a touch. Audrey had virtually nursed him into his present eminent position. Over the years he had eventually left all his affairs, domestic and private, to her management. He was the first to acknowledge his great fortune to possess such a devoted and highly practical wife. On the other hand, the fact that everyone invited to the conference had agreed to come at short notice, and at their own expense, was testament to Sir Henry's reputation.

"Darling, there's only one way to go about it. Start from the beginning, explain all your dealings with Louis, making it quite clear what he told you, then play the recording and let things take care of themselves."

"You're right as usual, my dear," said Henry. "Of course you must tell them of your experience with Louis as well, my darling. I can tell you I am not looking forward to this. It's too fantastic to think anyone will believe me, and yet that music must be explained."

"Must I tell of my visit to Louis?" asked Lady Audrey.

"Darling, of course you must. That misquote from Tennyson is most intriguing. If I am right, then he's in heaven too. I shall be most interested to hear what the great German conductors make of this mystery. Klemper is a stern, practical chap with not a bit of romance in him. I remember how startled he was when he heard the speed that Tartini took the eighth at. I'm sure those German imprecations are not to be found in the dictionary. How many are we expecting for the conference now?"

"I'll count them up," Audrey answered, as the telephone rang. "The Malcolm residence," said Audrey.

"This is Johnson of the *Times*, I wish to speak to Sir Henry. Am I speaking to Lady Audrey Malcolm?'

"You are."

"Lady Malcolm, you probably know my investigator Michael Lewis has been engaged on the Beynon story for weeks now and we're ready to go to press. We know just about everything, including your visit to him and, rather than cause a sensation, we would like to attend the conference as well."

"Why on earth should we? This is a private matter and of no concern to the papers."

"With respect, Lady Malcolm, it's nothing of the sort. It's of interest to the world and could I say to the very existence of the world. You see, we've read the message too. How far can I go in publishing it? That's the question." I held my breath waiting for her answer.

Lady Audrey thought for so long a time that I had to ask, "Are you there?"

"Yes, Mr. Johnson. I think you had better come and bring Mr. Lewis with you. But let me say at once that I want your word that you will treat the conference as absolutely confidential unless Sir Henry and the gathering committee determines otherwise."

"Very well, Lady Audrey. You have my word and thank you." Lady Audrey put the phone down slowly and stood motionless for some moments, deep in thought.

"Well, my dear, what was that all about?" asked Sir Henry.

"That was Mr. Johnson, Chief Editor of the *Times*, Henry, and he knows just about everything we do about Beynon. His man Lewis appears to have succeeded in tracing the source of the music and has placed the interpretation on it as you have. It would be foolish to antagonize them so I invited them to attend the conference after getting their word that nothing will be published without our consent."

"I see. Very well, darling. God knows what the outcome will be. We'll now have more people coming, plus now the press, plus those clergy invited by the Academy in Crete. We'll just have to see what reaction we get from these boffins and religious chaps."

Sir Henry and Lady Audrey devoted the rest of the day listening to the symphony again and again and studying the score. Henry made note after note about the various movements until he was satisfied that he could put his views across with ease. They thought of the academy in Crete where the conference would be held. They were a little apprehensive, never having been there before. A few days later they flew to Athens and then on to Crete for the conference. On the advice of the police, they left their South Kensington home in the dark of night bound for Heathrow where they boarded a flight to Athens, successfully avoiding any paparazzi. The inspector and I joined them at the academy on Crete a few hours later. Expectations were riding high.

The Island of Dreams

Sir Henry and Lady Malcolm arrived at Hania airport from Athens. The flight from London had been uneventful and they had both fallen asleep in the air. The academy had arranged for a car to pick them up at the airport and take them to the Christian Academy of Crete on the northwest coast of the island.

As the car sped along the coastal road, Lady Audrey's breath was taken away by the beautiful blue of the Mediterranean Sea and the rapidly changing scenery that was Crete. Noticing that Sir Henry's mood was again somber, Lady Audrey tried a diverting tactic.

"Look Henry, one minute the land is harsh and barren; the next, wooded and gentle; and that scent—fennel I think—and now there's basil wafting through the air."

Sir Henry obliged, "And see darling, too. There's a monastery perched on that mount as though it's about to fall down, straight into the underworld!"

Lady Audrey saw the monastery but looked away to search for the Cretan wild goats on the slopes of the island's massif that she had read symbolized the free spirit of Crete. *A free spirit is just what Henry needs now,* she thought, *never mind his underworld.*

Sir Henry suddenly found himself back in school where the stories of classical Greece were being imparted to impressionable young boys as imminent truth. Past and present were coalescing.

"Think, Audrey, this is the land of the Minoans who built palaces like Knossos; the land of Icarus who flew too close to the sun which melted the wax that held the feathers to his wings and crashed him into the sea where he drowned. And here was the labyrinth and the Minotaur, a monster with the body of a man and the head of a bull."

Lady Audrey noticed the spontaneous mental activity and smiled, "And Crete, Henry, was the birth place of El Greco, the master of Spanish painting who became the official painter of King Phillip of Spain in 1577. Yet his paintings are clearly a testament to the influence on him of Byzantine art. And this at the same time as King Phillip was preparing his armada to invade our England."

She thumbed again the pages in her guidebook, "This island is called the dream of Crete because here the spirit can soar in flight, a veritable island of miracles. I am glad we are here, Henry, on this beautiful and largest of all Greek islands. I have a good feeling about this conference. How about you, Henry? It is so beautiful here. It can't help but lift all our spirits up to sunny vistas."

"I trust you are right my dear. You usually are."

The driver took them into the Institute's offices where they were introduced to Dr. Andreas who was the Academy's director. Dr. Andreas greeted them warmly, showed them round the academy with all its facilities, and then to their room with a balcony overlooking the beautiful Mediterranean. All was most impressive and idyllic.

On the morning of the conference after breakfast they picked up their nametags and headed for the smaller conference room. Sir Henry looked to his wife as she spoke. "Go on dear, and now to business. Dr. Andreas will welcome everyone to the academy and then hand over proceedings to you, Henry. When they are all seated you can call their names and callings and that will constitute the formal introductions. Then you can begin by playing each movement to be followed by your interpretation. Perhaps you will have to play the first three or four times. After the music I take it the general discussions will follow. Lunch will be ready at one o'clock and dinner around 7:00 p.m. I am sure we will not disperse much before nine o'clock or 9:30. Tomorrow's proceedings will take care of themselves and will follow from what transpires today."

"Very well," said Sir Henry, "let's hope some explanation is possible from all these scientific and religious folk."

Half an hour later the first visitors arrived in the conference hall, soon to be followed by the remainder. Any ideas about formal introductions were rendered unnecessary by the meeting of many mutual friends and acquaintances. Coffee being available, the parties took to their seats and waited in keen anticipation for Dr. Andreas and Sir Henry to begin. JJ and the Inspector were the last to arrive, having just flown in with Paxton.

With Sir Henry standing by his side, Dr. Andreas welcomed everyone in accented but good English.

"It gives me great pleasure to welcome you all to The Christian Academy of Crete, and especially Sir Henry and Lady Audrey here.

"Before I hand over to Sir Henry I want to mention that the composer of the music you are about to hear came here to Crete and met with Fr. Papandreou, the Abbot and Head of the nearby monastery. It was Fr. Papandreou who, although he never heard the symphony you are about to hear, decided that a most unusual spiritual phenomenon was involved in its composing. Accordingly, Fr. Papandreou invited Sir Henry here to locate his conference here at the academy. So, Sir Henry, welcome and please let us begin."

Sir Henry stood up and waited as Lady Audrey handed to the musicians the only photocopies of the scores.

"Gentlemen," he said, "I give you each a copy of the score of the music you are about to hear, with the stipulation that all royalties must be donated to the musicians' benevolent fund in your own countries. The composer had no living relatives that we can find. However, there is a second stipulation that is potentially of far greater consequence. I will describe this second condition after we have all heard this 'mystery symphony' and discussed the interpretation. That will be near the end of the day. I explained to each of you when I called you, albeit rather briefly, why I would be grateful for your assistance in a most puzzling matter. There are two mysteries to clear up. I propose playing the recording of this symphony, but at the end of each movement I shall describe its meaning and interpretation as I see it and then invite the comments first of these famous conductors whom I am sure you have all recognized and then I shall ask you. This first movement is of very special significance and the next three I believe tell of a future at which my mind cannot grasp. The second mystery is the composer, but after the symphony has been played over I shall outline the extraordinary events leading up to my meeting with the composer Louis Beynon and to the 'mystery symphony's' first performance in London."

There were nods from all those present as the academy technician turned on the sound system and the "mystery symphony" started to play. While I looked blankly at the inspector, puzzled looks appeared on some faces but no words could describe the reaction of the musicians who stared at one another and shook their heads as if in total disbelief. Shock was an understatement if ever there was one, and almost simultaneously they rose as if to start an argument. I watched as Sir Henry glared at them and tacitly ordered them to sit down and wait. As the theme from Prometheus on the horns came clearly through the thunderous roll on the tympani, the conductors appeared to be startled, and remarks such as "*unmöglich*" and "impossible" were made.

As the movement drew to a close with a crashing coda Klemper and Richter were on their feet ready to question, but Sir Henry anticipating their questions stated flatly, "The composer, gentlemen, we will discuss at the end of the work. For now let us interpret the first movement. I'm sure you will have noticed some resemblance in this to the last movement of the ninth and even the Choral Fantasia, but only a suggestion. To me it was as if the doors of heaven were open for a moment and then that terrible atmosphere of a court with a judge about to sum up for the jury. Suddenly the judge has lost patience and, without recourse to the jury, pronounces sentence and orders it to be carried out immediately. It's as if God had weighed us in the balance and found us wanting. What follows at first made me think of Rome and Carthage and the horrible massacre of the third Punic War. Humanity had been wiped out and the world had become one huge necropolis. My mind was dwelling on a universal atomic war and the ultimate effects until that Prometheus theme pounded out its warning. As far as I am concerned, it's a clear indication that whatever destruction may come will be by some extraterrestrial action. I started to think of Velikowsky's theory about Venus and Exodus in the Bible and, frankly, I became a frightened man. Now then, who would like to speak first?"

Up jumped one cleric in Western attire, and in a slightly patronizing voice tempered with a little sarcasm, he remarked, "I cannot believe what you are construing here.

While appreciating your interpretation of picture painting, I do not see why there's such a fuss about a musical message. Must we all get into a state over some piece of music?"

I noticed that the inspector sitting next to me seemed sympathetic. He wanted to get up to give some support to this Western Bishop but I pulled him down and told him to wait his turn.

"But JJ, you brought me here to pursue the truth?"

"You'll get your turn like Sir Henry said. Be patient."

"Thank you, my Lord Bishop," replied Sir Henry in a slightly terse tone of voice. "Let us hear from our musician friends first, please." The other clerics understood that they would be called on after the musicians and conductors had expressed themselves.

Sir Thomas Boult, the great English conductor, stood up and remarked, "I agree about your reading of the music and were it not quite impossible, like our German friends I would say it's Beethoven at his mightiest. Obviously there is a great deal more to come and I wait entranced, but very puzzled."

As nobody else volunteered any further comment, Sir Henry nodded to the technician and the music continued. The slow movement began. It was apparent to most from the start that this was a Requiem Mass and a deeply penetrating one at that. The listeners sat frozen in their seats as the intense sorrow and at times anger and rage registered on their emotions. In typical Beethoven style the mood changed and one got the feeling of a void and the endless passing of millions of years. There was an unbearable nothingness; all life had passed into the limbo of forgotten things. The tempo quickened slightly with the sudden re-entry of the four sopranos singing in unison what was patently a prayer of supplication of the most heavenly beauty around which the violins wove a very delicate variation. This theme was taken up by the full orchestra as the slow movement moved into the scherzo without a break. By now the intense character of the music had gripped most of the audience. JJ noticed that even the inspector sat motionless with a decidedly puzzled look on his face.

All the musicians expressed utter concentration. There could be no doubt but that their interest was not only in the quality of the music but also in something else deeply disturbing and inexplicable. Richter and Klemper displayed horror coupled with extreme disbelief only to relapse again and again into resignation. Quite definitely the inner meaning of all this wonderful music had bitten deeply. Tartini seemed about to explode. Here was no Italian intrigue but a solid statement of fact and intention. The British conductors scarcely moved. Nevertheless, there was that British expression of doggedness and backs to the wall. With them too, the meaning of the symphony was perfectly clear. They waited patiently for some expected climax; the picture was drawing to its ultimate end wherein the fate of mankind was to be determined.

The scherzo ended on a long, drawn out shriek of agony, which served to indicate that a terrible decision had been made. Sir Henry looked at his audience yet again and finally asked Sir Thomas whether he would like to comment on his reactions to the second and third movements.

"I speak only for myself, Sir Henry, and yet I can almost sense that our friends here have read this as I have. The second movement is a Requiem Mass for the passing of mankind," said Sir Thomas to the emphatic nods from his colleagues, "Then follows what I can only describe as the endless passing of time, say thousands if not millions of years. The entry of the sopranos is much like their entry in the Choral Fantasia and there can be no doubt that they are begging for God to permit the rebirth of mankind. The words themselves in German 'Forgive them Lord, their ignorance of love is beyond our understanding' makes this quite clear. These angels I shall call them are beseeching God to relent and that sudden entry into the scherzo signifies to me His impatience and determination that His sentence has been given and that appeals will be of no avail. Perhaps Herr Professor Richter would be good enough to give his views on the third movement. I have mine, but I would welcome other opinions," and Sir Thomas sat down.

Richter moved slowly and it was patently obvious that he, too, was suffering from an emotional disturbance. "Yes, Sir Thomas. Never have I heard such disturbing music. This can only be Beethoven but as we know this is impossible, but Sir Henry has asked us not to speak of the composer until we have heard the whole symphony. So, for the scherzo I say Sir Thomas' interpretation of the slow movement is as mine and in the scherzo God refuses to consider allowing mankind another chance to live. God recalls all the horrors which man has penetrated in His name. He reminds himself of the centuries of massacres, tortures, murders, and beastliness all carried out 'for Him.'

Souls were 'saved' by burning people alive! People who worshipped in a way different from those in power were declared heretics and destroyed in His name. There was no tolerance. Religion was a political expedient always in the name of God. No religion is free of guilt in His view. He has made his decision that man is a prehistoric creature and that the universe will suffer no loss for his extinction. I can hardly wait to hear the last movement. There will only be one more movement, Sir Henry, yes?" And Richter sat down to a nod from Sir Henry.

"Very well, gentlemen; we shall now play the final movement and after interpretation we shall pass to the most intriguing and puzzling aspect of this composition—its composer," said Sir Henry.

Sir Henry nodded to the technician and the music started again. The movement opened 'con fuoco,' the chords crashing as the violins raced into prestissimo only to stop suddenly. Then followed a series of hesitations, once more to be resolved into a furious outburst that finally receded as the orchestra strings introduced a slow, agonizingly beautiful new motif.

Once more, slight hesitations and then a wonderful triumphant march in which every instrument of the orchestra played fortissimo. It was clear at this point that the movement had entered the coda and as the music softened before entering the final phase of the triumphant march, very clearly and emphatically the motif of the fifth symphony penetrated the beautiful larghetto on the strings. With a short recapitulation of the march, the symphony ended with a typical but original crashing run from the base to the

ERIK ERIKSSON

96

highest pitch, which left the listeners in a state of ecstasy. As the music finished, Sir Henry rose to his feet and, turning to the greatest authority on Beethoven in this era asked, "I should like my old friend Herr Professor Klemper to comment only on the music at this stage please."

"Sir Henry, gentlemen, Your Excellencies, and Lord Bishops, and of course Lady Audrey, now I understand at last why my friend Professor Ries was so amazed in Vienna a few weeks ago. He was listening to the broadcast from London after being asked by you, Sir Henry. I thought he had gone mad when he told me that I wouldn't believe what I would hear today. I too must be mad because this can only be Beethoven—nobody, but nobody I say, but Beethoven wrote this. But you ask me to say what this last movement means. I agree with what our friends have said about the first three movements and the reading of the fourth follows logically. God strides across the heavens, pondering whether man should be given another chance to people the earth. He doubts that man deserves this chance but much against His better judgment finally gives way to the pleas from those in Heaven and relents. Man shall be given that chance once again. Then comes that wonderful march and to me the gates of heaven open once again and the life force returns to Earth. The second Genesis is to begin. He hesitates once or twice, as if He would stop this Exodus, but he gives way."

In the coda, as you heard, the march gloriously rearranged is interrupted in the most sinister way by a very, very, cold introduction of the motif of the fifth symphony. He warns man that his fate will be determined by his own actions and that this is his last and only chance. Like you, Sir Malcolm, I believe the world will be destroyed and there is nothing we can do about it. The message is clear that God has decided that man is lower than the animals and has to be removed from creation," and Klemper sat down.

Up shot the same Western Bishop once more in a sarcastic tone of voice, "This is sure blasphemy! How can you musicians say this of God and His ways just from some, well, some piece of music?" Other Bishops and clerics wanted to speak, but Sir Henry gestured that they would get their turn very soon.

"Thank you my Lord Bishop, you will pardon me if I call that title a little blasphemous. Musicians first, please." But the inspector jumped up to speak, not being able to resist any more.

"But Sir Henry, how can you say all this from some piece of music? The Bishop has a point."

I wished the inspector had been less spontaneous. Not wanting to get Sir Henry's ire up, I turned to remonstrate with him but Sir Henry got there first.

"Mr. Lewis, please, your turn will come," replied Sir Henry.

"But Sir Henry—" The inspector protested at not being able to finish his sentence. I quietly grabbed him. "Michael, please sit down and wait your turn."

Sir Henry continued, "Let us leave personalities out and try to be objective. I am now going to outline my association with Louis Beynon, the composer of this work which by the way he utterly denied, and I hope, my Lord Bishop, that you understand His mysterious ways because you will have your chance to have your say."

The Bishop shrugged his shoulders in a resigned way. "These naïve children" and subsided into his chair. Sir Henry's facial expression clearly showed that he wondered what this Bishop was doing at the conference.

Very slowly and impassively Sir Henry began to outline his connection with Louis Beynon and this work confirming a lot of what the inspector and I already knew. He started with his quite accidental hearing of the first rehearsal and Beynon's remarks and behavior with the Royal Academy of Music orchestra leading up ultimately to the first performance at Festival Hall.

"I realized," Sir Henry continued, "that there was something beyond my understanding, not the musical content only but what our friends so often call the inner meaning. However, I wish you to hear Professor Paxton outline his connection with Beynon."

Paxton related at great length his dealings with Beynon and added, "Time and time again, while Louis Beynon denied composing this music, I tried to get some direct reply as to the real composer but it was obvious that he could not accept nor understand what was happening. But every remark, every unguarded reply, indicated Beethoven. And gentlemen, crazy as it appears, that's my view," and Paxton sat down.

Sir Henry rose once again. "Oh, no, gentlemen, there's a great deal more. I was lucky enough to speak to Doctor Jacobs and Mrs. Todd. Dr. Jacobs was looking after him and Mrs. Todd was his landlady." Sir Henry read from his notes and Beynon's comments were given verbatim. "One thing more, and this may interest our scientific friends." He then gave his audience an account of Beynon's visit to the medium and ended with "I make no comment, I merely relate the facts as given by Miss Billson who teaches the violin at the Royal Academy of Music. Now Mr. Lewis, you have been chomping at the bit, wanting to speak further. I understand you have been making independent inquiries for the *Times* newspaper. Would you like to add anything?"

The inspector outlined in some detail the results of his inquiries and ended, "That, gentlemen, was as far as I could get. I must now say that I am no wiser now that Sir Henry has told us all he knows."

"Not quite all, Mr. Lewis, but go on, please," interjected Sir Henry.

"There's not much left, Sir Henry. As a journalist and investigator, I was faced with a choice between believing many highly regarded people were deliberate liars or just plain deluded, including these famous conductors here and yourself, Sir Henry; or, telling the world that there is a heaven in which not only were Beethoven and others in residence as it were, but that God, through Beethoven, had sent His warning to mankind that He was about to destroy the world. Frankly, I got drunk. If I had to choose between the two I would say that it is more likely that these musicians and yourself, Sir Henry, are either deliberately lying or you are all deluded." And with that the inspector sat down, as though that's what he did every day.

I could hardly believe my ears that the inspector had been so rude in his choice of words. Like me, the conductors were on the edge of their seats wondering how Sir Henry would deal with this insult.

Sir Henry got to his feet retaining his composure.

"Well, thank you for your candor, Mr. Lewis. I do believe you are here because your boss Mr. Johnson asked Lady Audrey if he could bring you. I do believe an apology is called for since you are our guest here."

The inspector had been put in his place. He noticed that I, his boss, was noticeably angry with him.

"Don't you ever be rude and discourteous like that again, Michael. What were you thinking about? We are here to get at the truth and a story for *The Times*. Now kindly apologize."

Michael turned away and kept quiet. I understood why Scotland Yard had wanted him transferred. One more outburst like that and I would fire him myself! From what I had heard and read, the inspector and Beethoven had one thing in common. They were both spontaneous in giving their comments and sometimes without any regard for the consequences, and neither would apologize when asked.

"Michael, apologize. Sir Henry is waiting."

But the inspector did not get up nor apologize.

Sir Henry delivered the blow.

"Well then, I think you will remove yourself from these proceedings." And with that Sir Henry looked away and went on. Had Michael now blown it for *The Times?*

"Well, now you have done it, Michael. You'd better walk out and go back to your room. You'd better hope that Sir Henry will allow you back in when you are ready to apologize. Go on, go!" And with that the inspector left the auditorium in disgrace.

"Now, where were we? Ah, yes. My wife, Lady Audrey, was present at Louis Beynon's death and I now leave her to tell you what happened."

Lady Audrey, who had been listening intently to all that had gone before, rose shyly and self-consciously to address a gathering that somehow reminded her of her first solo performance as a pianist before a distinguished concert audience at Queen's Hall. Only this time she could not immediately address herself to the piano and regard her listeners as so many fish on a slab. These people were highly intelligent and their concentrated looks gave her a feeling of inadequacy. Taking a deep breath she began, "I met Louis some years ago when he first came to the Academy and, of course, on many other occasions when they held parties and concerts. He was very friendly and, as he was a bachelor, I tried to help him with his small domestic problems. In fact, I got him his apartment at Mrs. Todd's place and for some reason he was inordinately grateful. A few weeks ago he rang me asking if I would go and see him but I explained that Sir Henry and I would be in Edinburgh for the festival and that I would come and see him on my return. He seemed worried about something but said no more. I am very sorry to say that on our return I heard that he was ill so I rushed around to his flat. Mrs. Todd and Dr. Jacobs were there at the time and I was informed that he was very weak and almost unconscious. I sat at his bedside for some time hoping that he might recover and speak to me."

Lady Audrey paused and then resumed, "You can imagine my utter surprise when he suddenly said, 'I don't think they realize that it is ordained but I've done my best—yes, yes I shall repeat it, but it's not correct, but if you say so' and then very slowly he said as if repeating something being said by another, 'We dipped into the future far as every eye could see, saw the vision of the world and all the horror that would be; saw the heavens fill with naptha and there rained a ghastly dew, as nation after nation disappeared from you.'"

With that he passed into a coma and died that evening. Dr. Jacobs gave the cause of death as heart failure from physical and mental exhaustion but added that he still could not understand what brought it all about. I was then told by Mrs. Todd of his nocturnal activities and now you know as much as I do."

She sat down and utter silence reigned in the room. Sir Henry rose after a few minutes and said, "Well, I can tell you emphatically that Beynon did not compose this music." The musicians nodded their approval with Sir Henry's statement. "He received it from somewhere, if that's the right expression. Perhaps your deep understanding of the mysterious ways of the almighty can assist us, my Lord?"

The Western Bishop scowled at Sir Henry as he replied, "Are you asking me to believe that up there or out there somewhere there is some place where departed souls gather, such as the dead and gone musicians who compose music and pass it on to people on earth?"

"And apparently poets; Tennyson for one, if those corrupted lines mean anything," retorted Sir Henry.

"Preposterous," said the Western Bishop, "a musical message from Heaven, and delivered ready for performance; really, how preposterous!"

One of the Orthodox priests stood up and, looking towards the Western Bishop, spoke softly in broken English, "Why not, my Lord? Isn't this what Jesus and the church have taught for centuries, that the kingdom of Heaven is within us and that we are to seek it before all else and then all will be added unto us? We know that God is close. So those who have found the kingdom of Heaven will be close too, whether alive in this world or passed on, and also able to guide and help those who are still seeking."

Sir Henry suddenly started to feel the same inner force and excitement that he had felt when conducting "the mystery symphony" at the Royal Festival Hall.

The Western Bishop quickly retorted, "That may be, Your Excellency. But a God of love does not threaten his creation with extinction. Scripture does not endorse that, and certainly not the New Testament."

The Greek Bishop replied, "But what we are hearing here today is human interpretation of the music and not that of the divine. That's the difference. Not one of these famous conductors is claiming to have found the kingdom of Heaven."

The Greek Bishop looked at all the conductors and found every one of them nodding with approval.

"The Divine interpretation may be quite different."

The Western Bishop was on the spot, "No, I am not saying that I speak for Heaven either. But then are you saying that Beethoven entered into the kingdom of

Heaven and therefore is now able to guide others? He was certainly no saint according to the history books. In fact, I have read that he was cantankerous, judgmental, and decidedly superior in his attitude towards others. He lacked tolerance. All his reactions were violent and direct. These are not human characteristics that suggest beatification. Heaven with an orchestra and Beethoven, poets, and goodness knows what; it's ridiculous."

Like all the conductors present, Sir Thomas was not amused at these judgmental comments about Beethoven. He wondered if this Bishop had ever created anything.

"My Lord Bishop, please, listen to what Richard Wagner wrote about Beethoven's music. It just might help you to understand, 'Who does not hear the Redeemer's word when listening to the Pastoral symphony? And…Thus these wonderful works preach repentance and atonement in the deepest sense of divine revelation.'"

An Eastern cleric stood up to speak, "My Lord Bishop, you say that he lacked tolerance; but he also lacked the ability to be cynical, and so was direct in his tone and approach. Surely, no man was ever more true to his own experience than was Beethoven; and no man was ever less ashamed of himself than was Beethoven. These are great spiritual virtues and decidedly necessary for the appearance of genius. If we had suffered, as did Beethoven, from a growing deafness and poor general health as well as being harshly treated as a child raised in near poverty, perhaps we might have been sometimes grumpy and belligerent. Surely, it is God who makes saints and raises them up to His level because of a man or woman's inner parts and motives. Maybe we clergy don't always get it right, because we so often focus on the outer behavior. What about his music? The beautiful music that Beethoven wrote in his ninth symphony to Schiller's 'Ode to Joy' would certainly suggest that Beethoven had found favor with God and entered into paradise or Elysium. Just listen!"

He then read out the words of Schiller's "Ode to Joy" and Sir Henry played a few bars from the last movement of the ninth symphony. There was an air of surprise yet nodding agreement from many of the clerics in the room with these comments.

A hand went up to speak, but not from a cleric.

Sir Henry rose quickly and said, "Gentlemen, gentlemen, we have here an American, Mr. Carl Larson, who is a great-grandson of the famous author Christian Larson who wrote many books on spiritual subjects in the early 1900s. Mr. Larson, please give us your thoughts from 'The New World.' We are all eager to hear you."

"Thank you, Sir Henry, for mentioning my great-grandfather Christian Larson who was part of the New Thought movement in the early twentieth century. A special thanks must go to the Orthodox Church for inviting me here." Mr. Larson gestured his sincere thanks as he turned to where most of the Eastern Orthodox clergy were seated and bowed to them.

"I would like to concur with what our orthodox friends have said and go a little further, adding what my grandfather taught more than seventy-five years ago. In one of his many books my grandfather gave some guidelines for finding the way to freedom and those paths that leads to the life beautiful."

He then read out those verses.

"Now I know that my orthodox colleagues here are well familiar with St Paul's injunction 'to pray without ceasing' since this is so beautifully explained in that classic book of Russian spirituality called *The Way of A Pilgrim*." The Eastern clerics nodded.

"My grandfather taught that the great things in life do not come through minds that are dominated by the reports of the everyday world that make it to the six o'clock news. Rather, everything new and of real worth has come through the mind that can have great dreams and rise to great inner heights. To be practical is, of course, necessary. But the practical does not come first, and cannot act until the vision or idea has been apprehended. You may be familiar with the words to this effect of Eleanor Roosevelt:

'The future belongs to those who believe in the beauty of their dreams.'"

That Mr. Larson was getting everybody's attention was clear. There was an active silence in the air, a pregnant expectation.

"Now we have been told how to do this. We are to go within by closing the door to our everyday problems, concerns, and to the radio and T.V. We are to be still, and to know with faith that God is present. We are to think about God—how loving, how tolerant, how merciful He is, and then we are to take to Him what we have in mind and what we want. We are to thank God for what we have in mind, and with a thankful heart and attitude, to know, with faith and not doubting, that we have already been given it. My grandfather taught that it is in touching our desires in this state of attunement that is the key to having our prayers answered and our desires materialize in the world. This is the technique."

That Beethoven regularly entered the spiritual silence perhaps more than most others is as obvious as it later was dreadful for him when this was overshadowed by his physical deafness, at least until he accepted his deafness and had a change of heart."

Mr. Larson went on, "So here we have this beautiful 'mystery symphony' that came to this man Louis Beynon who, from what I have heard here, readily acknowledged that he did not compose it as other composers do, but rather got it from on high or from these finer realms. Since there seems to be no question that it is great music, whether by Beethoven or not, there would seem to be no doubt that it does come from on high, from these fine, beautiful realms."

Now, I can only guess that the head of the monastery, Fr. Papandreou, came to this conclusion himself and that that is why he invited Sir Henry to have this conference here."

You could have heard a pin drop, just as was the case when Sir Henry had conducted the "mystery symphony" at The Royal Festival Hall.

Although Mr. Larson had expanded on what the orthodox clerics had said, he had taken the discussion out of the domain of conventional religion. This was patently evident, even to me, a philistine.

He had moved it into the realm of a science or art of living and concentration, where a cleric's vocation would be more to show people how to do this and to inspire them to live the truth through example, as of course did Jesus and his disciples. Some of the clergy present seemed to realize this immediately, some were still thinking about it. Some were comfortable with this, thinking they should be doing this anyway. Others were not, wondering if they could. Mr. Larson ended with, "The real question, ladies and gentlemen, is what the divine interpretation is of this 'mystery symphony.'" And with that, Mr. Larson sat down.

The room was pregnant with anticipation. The situation had been turned upside down. The conductors no longer had to believe that the destruction of the world was imminent, yet it was agreed that "the mystery symphony" was genuinely inspired from on high. The Western Bishop was vindicated too.

Sir Henry did not want to lose the moment. He rose straightaway to speak:

"I would like now to call upon Mr. Bruce whom I'm told is a high dignitary of the Buddhist faith. While I confess an absolute ignorance of their religion, I seem to remember reading of a girl in India who astounded the scientists out there by proving that she had lived before. She was able to give details of this previous life in a far away village to which she had never been. There was never a satisfactory answer given. I wanted to ask Mr. Bruce whether their reincarnation beliefs could accept that Beynon was Beethoven reincarnated?"

Mr. Bruce, who personified the very spirit of asceticism, slowly got to his feet.

"I know, Sir Henry, you do not wish me to deliver a long dissertation on my faith, and especially in this beautiful Christian academy. I will say that while we believe that the souls of the departed return to a new life at a level determined by their previous lives I cannot possibly identify the past soul with a present being. Let me say that it is entirely possible. But I should mention to you that in our way of looking at things, Jesus' statement 'there are many mansions in my father's house' could just as easily refer to the fact that each individual has many 'houses' that represent the personalities from each previous incarnation. The personality from the last incarnation would tend to be the most dominant in the sub-conscious mind. That's all I can really say on the matter, Sir Henry."

"Thank you, Mr. Bruce," replied Sir Henry. "Now then, I think most of you will have heard of a lady called Mrs. Rosemary Brown who it is reported has been in touch with the great composers of the past. She has, we're told, been writing compositions dictated to her by Beethoven, Lizst, Mozart, and so on. The report is that these departed masters are in touch and she puts their music on paper. Now, I have heard many of these so-called 'classics' and can only say that if indeed these composers did write these works, I'm not surprised that they were not published during their lifetime because most of what I've listened to is just so much noise in the style of so and so as it were. Anyone can copy something."

Sir Henry asked several scientists in ESP and psychic research for their comments but none were able to contribute anything significant, especially after the words of Mr. Larson.

Sir Henry rose slowly and addressing the whole gathering stated, "Well, now, I think it is time for us to break for dinner." There were nods from everyone. "Ah yes, but before you go I must speak to the conductors here about the second stipulation that I referred to at the beginning of this conference. You have received from my wife this morning a copy of the 'mystery symphony.'"

You will remember that I said that it was potentially of far greater significance than the first, which was that all royalties be donated to the Musicians' Benevolent Fund in your own countries."

"I have carefully watched all your reactions to hearing this 'mystery symphony' today and listened to your comments. Like me, you have been seriously troubled by this wonderful yet disturbing composition, the divine meaning notwithstanding. There is obviously a chance that future performances of this mystery symphony may lead again to considerable fear and anxiety in the general population. Before coming here I met with a famous physicist and astronomer. He tells me that there is a real chance for an extraterrestrial collision around 2012, but that about one hundred years from now there is something in the heavens that could, in his opinion, if not modified in some way, eradicate life on our planet as we know it. He will not publish his findings. You will appreciate that most people and governments will not want to let the world be destroyed if they actually come somehow to believe this message! Now, America's 'Star Wars' program may be sufficient to modify it, if not actually avert this threat, but we really don't know if this is true. The second stipulation is therefore this." All the conductors present were now on the edges of their seats!

"After one public performance of this 'Beethoven' symphony in your own countries you will gauge public reaction. If you conclude that the likelihood of increasing panic and anxiety in the general population is too great, you will give no more public performances of this mystery symphony and will secure the one manuscript that I have given you and place it in safe keeping, or return it to me. You will, of course, make no additional copies of the script and will not allow anyone else to see or 'borrow' the manuscript. We must act responsibly here and not be the instruments of panic in the world. I will call each of you in the near future; and if this is to be our course of action and, assuming we are in substantial agreement on this, I will, like you, make plans for my original copy of the manuscript to effectively disappear. To the general public, the manuscript will have disappeared and be just another component in this mystery."

Gentlemen, is this acceptable to you? If so, may I have your assurance that you will respect this request and take the proper measures accordingly?"

There was general agreement that this was the responsible thing to do. Many were clearly troubled by Sir Henry's report of a possible extraterrestrial cataclysm to come. They had felt this in the music.

"However, I see that I am being given a message to read to you. Ah yes, ladies and gentlemen, it is from Father Papandreou, head of the nearby monastery. He says that he will be able to be with us after dinner and that he will speak to us. Well, I for one look forward to this and I am sure that you all do too. It is because of him that we are here on this beautiful island and in this enlightened academy. We will reassemble in just over one hour." And with that Sir Henry invited everyone to follow him to dinner.

Noticing me in the corridors. Sir Henry stopped to talk, "One thing please, Mr. Johnson; I do not propose to talk to the press and I cannot dictate to you, but I hope you will agree to regard this meeting as highly confidential and give no clue as to its purpose nor quote any individual's comments. I trust this will apply to your Mr. Lewis too." I nodded my agreement.

"Now, gentlemen I hope you will join us all for dinner." Sir Henry motioned to his wife as they moved towards the dining room.

The evening meal came and went and it was clear from the small talk that all were keenly looking forward to hearing Fr. Papandreou speak after supper.

Sir Henry welcomed the tall, thin, bearded Father who was characteristically attired all in black with that typical Eastern Orthodox headpiece which he proceeded to adjust before beginning to speak.

But who walked in with him, arm in arm, but the inspector! How did this happen? Everyone was shocked to see this after his insulting behavior. Evidently Fr. Papandreou had been talking to him outside.

It was clear the inspector had found an ally in the head of the monastery, and an important one. Michael looked noticeably contrite with his head hanging down, yet this seemed more out of respect for the good Father, as though this man of God had taken him under his wing. JJ wondered if the inspector was about to find religion. The inspector's "time out" was obviously over. Had Lady Luck arrived?

Fr. Papandreou thanked Sir Henry and welcomed all to the academy again as the inspector stood by his side.

"Inspector Lewis told me of his overzealous behavior and poor choice of words as we met outside. I told him that he was one person that I knew needed to be here, and not only for his own sake. Many are indeed called, as we know, but few choose to accept the Master's correction that leads to the soul's ascent to God. He has apologized to me, which I have accepted on your behalf. I trust this is satisfactory to you, Sir Henry, and to you, Lady Audrey, and to the other famous conductors here."

JJ could hardly believe his ears. The implication of these comments was clear. The inspector had apparently accepted God's correction. JJ was taken aback.

Did this abbot just say that the inspector had to be here, and for God's purpose? Does this mean that the inspector has found favor with God?

JJ looked directly at Michael.

He wondered where this would all lead. Was the inspector going to get God's help in finding out if Beethoven was now in heaven writing new symphonies for God?

Is this possible?

Everybody nodded that this was satisfactory, and the inspector certainly looked relieved. It was clear that Fr. Papandreou had excellent personal skills and would make a great arbitrator. All in the room felt at ease. But it was more than this. He had a presence which could be sensed as you looked at him. Such was the changing atmosphere in the room.

The inspector sat down next to me in his old seat, but kept his eyes to himself, not noticing that I was no longer angry with him.

Fr. Papandreou then read out the following quote:

"'The most beautiful and most profound emotion we can experience is the sensation of the mystical. It is the sewer of all true science. He to whom this emotion is a stranger, who can no longer wonder and stand rapt in awe, is as good as dead. To know that what is impenetrable to us really exists, manifesting itself as the highest wisdom and the most radiant beauty which our dull faculties can understand only in their most primitive forms—this knowledge, this feeling, is at the center of true religiousness.'"

I suddenly realized myself that the good Father himself looked rapt in awe, and that he was indeed someone quite special.

"Now who do you think wrote this, ladies and gentlemen? Was it some great theologian or saint?" He waited to see if anyone in the audience would reply but no one did.

"Perhaps we should answer 'yes' in some sense, but most people would have said 'no,' since these words were written by Albert Einstein, a scientist and modern-day genius. Yet surely these words apply equally to Beethoven, who wrote his emotive words of wisdom in music. I have been doing some research. The words of George Bernard Shaw probably give us one of the best insights into Beethoven's life:

> 'Beethoven was the first man who used music with absolute integrity as the expression of his own emotional life … Beethoven made this, and nothing else, his business … In thus fearlessly expressing himself, he has, by his common humanity, expressed us as well, and shown us how beautifully, how strongly, how trustworthily we can build with our own real selves … In this light all Beethoven's work becomes clear and simple; and the old nonsense about his obscurity and eccentricity and stage sublimity and so on explains itself as pure misunderstanding …'"

I am sure you will understand then that the goals of this academy embrace science and religion equally, and their common ground, as you have heard from Dr. Andreas.

Fr. Papandreou went on: "It seems clear to me that like Beethoven, Albert Einstein was well familiar with entering the silence and pulling out treasures that were waiting for him. After all, they were relative(s) as you will agree!"

Everyone laughed and immediately felt at ease with this delightful man. I noticed that the inspector was clearly taken with him. He looked as though he had found some long lost relative.

"Well, nearly half a year ago, I met Louis Beynon when he stayed at the monastery for one week. He was quite troubled by what he was experiencing, as you can imagine. His mother was half Greek and a devout Orthodox Christian whose family was originally from this island of Crete. After the German invasion of Crete in World War II, the mother's family joined the Greek resistance movement while this monastery again became a target for attack by the invaders and was partially destroyed by them. As if this was not dangerous enough, several of the men in the family were members of Masonic lodges and on the Nazis' list for extermination. My predecessors at the monastery hid the family and many got out later and moved to London. One brother, however, did not go with them and became a monk at this monastery. So it was not unexpected that Louis would come here when his mind was literally invaded by this great orchestral symphony. It was like a spiritual home to the family."

A hand went up from Mr. Larson.

"Fr. Papandreou, if I may, have you heard the 'mystery symphony'?"

"No, I never heard the music that he was describing while he was here. Yet from his comments it was clearly magnificent, awesome, and terrifying in places. He asked me about the voices he heard, and especially that of Beethoven. He wanted reassurance that he was not going mad. I told him that he did not have any signs of madness. In fact, apart from the music that was flooding into him he did not seem that odd; eccentric, yes."

The western Bishop got up to speak.

"Father Papandreou, what led you to think that there was something worthy of investigation here, if you had not heard the music itself?"

Fr. Papandreou bowed to the Western Bishop.

"I won't go into the details here Your Grace, but after considerable prayer about it, both separately and with Louis Beynon, I came to the conclusion that this was a genuine spiritual phenomenon that needed to be investigated properly. He told me that he had tried hard as a teenager to reach up to God. So I replied that perhaps this beautiful new symphony was the result of God reaching down to him in return, that the Creator had now found him and so was able to create through him, giving him this beautiful music. He certainly liked this idea, but he always wondered if he was truly listening to the dead Beethoven speak. He said that if these voices were not from Beethoven in heaven, who or what were they? I said that I did not know, but that perhaps we could find out."

The Western Bishop was wondering about the source of these voices, but decided to hold off asking his questions till later.

"After Mr. Beynon returned to England I entered the silence of my own heart as we all do here regularly. I thanked God for the proper investigation into this 'mystery symphony' that I had decided was warranted and which needed to be fruitful and informative when it took place. Later on, when I heard that this 'mystery symphony' had actually been performed in London conducted by Sir Henry here, I called him and offered to host here at the Academy what he was already planning. He accepted, and here we all are."

The inspector was clearly impressed with the good Father, especially with his idea of investigating this remarkable phenomenon. Before I could stop him he stood up to speak. Even though momentarily I thought to stop him, yet just as fast, I just knew that all would be okay now, that he was not going to insult anyone anymore.

"Fr. Papandreou, if I may ask, how do you propose to investigate this mystery? Actually there are two mysteries. One is the great music itself with its stirring and awesome message, and the other is the composer who apparently did not compose it at all, and who in any event is now dead. Is this not something of a challenge?"

"Well, Mr. Lewis, I am glad that you have asked this. From your own comments and profession is this not why you yourself were invited here? May we rely on you bringing your professional skills, and especially your purpose, to this investigation of Beethoven and this 'mystery symphony'?"

A light came on in JJ's head when Fr. Papandreou said 'your purpose.'

"So that was it. God is going to help the inspector check out this 'mystery symphony.'" JJ held his breath. He saw The Times headlines in front of his eyes!

The inspector again felt personally put in his place, but now, in a positive way, as though he was honor bound to do his best. He soon realized, though, that the investigation had now been formally handed over to him in public. His reputation and that of Scotland Yard were now on the line. He remembered, just in time, that I, his boss, was next to him!

"Subject to the approval of my chief here, Mr. Johnson, yes Fr. Papandreou."

I stood up and added, "If it's not a lengthy investigation, I don't see a problem."

Seeing that I was no longer angry, Michael turned and whispered.

"JJ look! Do you see how bright this good Father is?"

"Michael, he obviously is very smart. He tamed *you*!"

"No, I don't mean that, JJ. Look at his face and head. He is glowing like a light bulb! I can hardly look, the light is so bright!"

"I don't see that, Michael, but there is something special about him, that's for sure."

"Wow, look at those violet and white beams of light shooting out of his head. Good heavens, what is that … ?"

JJ could hear the inspector's newly found enthusiasm and signaled to him his warm approval.

"Okay Michael, let's just listen!"

Fr. Papandreou continued, "Gentlemen, this is what I propose, while we are all here, to set the ball rolling so to speak. I am going to sit here and go into the silence of the heart as we regularly do here. By way of my purpose in doing so, I am going to thank God for helping all of us to understand better these two mysteries. I invite you all to do the same with me."

Everybody was most surprised, but no one got up to leave. It was as though it was quite natural. Fr. Papandreou continued, "The first thing to do is to sit comfortably and relax. Turn your thoughts inwards towards the Creator at the center of your being. Let go of your awareness of this room, and let yourself become aware of the presence of God as you rise up to meet Him. Then, think of this 'mystery symphony' and any connection to Beethoven. Be thankful, and be still. The rest will take care of itself."

JJ remained wide awake. He decided to watch. Many followed the good Father's invitation and drifted off. The inspector was off too. But where had he gone? If he understood Fr. Papandreou, the inspector was off tuning into God's purpose, checking out Beethoven's life and this 'mystery symphony.' JJ recalled that Beethoven was always falling in love. He wondered how important his aristocratic lady friends were to him. The inspector was about to find out.

♪

Countess Anna Marie Erdödy was playing the piano in front of her husband Count Peter, endeavoring to relax and gain her strength back now that they had three children. She suddenly stopped and lurched forward onto the keys. Seeing his wife's distress, the Count got up in a timely manner to help her onto the nearby sofa and called for the Countess's lady in waiting. "It's all right," replied Anna Marie. "I just had that sharp pain in my side and leg again. It's a little better now."

"I have invited 'Mr. Beethoven' to come my dear. He will be here a little later today. Perhaps you will play his latest piano works to entertain him, being such an accomplished pianist yourself. I have to go to attend to some business at the theater."

As her husband said this, Anna Marie sensed they would eventually live apart. He had not said anything but somehow she thought this was her husband's wish. Her illness and periodic pain since the birth of their first child had put a strain on their marriage that was ongoing. But it was now more than this.

The Countess's family were hereditary trustees of an ancient society with traditions and scripts that went back to Ancient Egypt. It also had its 'mysteries.' The Countess called it her 'Isis temple.' The family duty had now fallen to the Countess herself to ensure its continuance and good standing. Count Peter was not sympathetic to this.

"My dear, I hear from my friends that Napoleon Bonaparte will soon be appointed the new Grand Master of your society in France. You say it is not a political society but you may rest assured that he will make it so. Times have changed. I think it would be appropriate for you to withdraw from it for your good name and mine."

"That, I cannot do, Peter. This has been a hereditary responsibility of my family for more than five hundred years. I will not allow one French Emperor to alter my family's proud trusteeship of what is a noble, time-honored, and purely spiritual fraternity. As you know, it is devoted to the raising of the spiritual part of man and nothing else. I would be depriving our children of their future duties."

"Well then, let us forget that, and prepare for the arrival of 'Mr. Beethoven.' You will surely be able to comfort him in his growing deafness, my dear. He will be most appreciative."

The Count and Countess were both correct. In a little while, 'Mr. Beethoven' would indeed be facing a crisis in his life as the onset of his deafness kept on coming.

"Ludwig, why don't we go for a walk in the countryside? You love it so dearly."

"But my dear," said Ludwig, "should you be walking when you know it will surely make your discomfort worse?"

"Ludwig, don't let's talk about my pain, let's talk about you. You're the one who is so down these days."

Beethoven started to deny it, preferring to talk about her life rather than have to face himself.

"Now don't try and fool me, Ludwig. This approaching deafness is taking its toll on you."

Ludwig noticed she had said '*this* deafness' most sympathetically and not just 'your deafness.'

"So you really care." He put his hand on hers. She did not take her hand away.

"Of course I care," replied the Countess. Just then the children came running in to see this moment of intimacy. The Countess did not hide from it and gently spoke to them.

"Just go and play now children. Mr. Beethoven is talking about his hearing problems."

"You know my dear, dear Countess, I remember when I was a young boy in Bonn. I would look up to the heavens over the Rhine and be enthralled by the magic of it all. Often I would feel that I was drifting off somewhere else, somewhere beautiful, away from my father's brutality and drunkenness. It was 'there' that I first saw my purpose or destiny to write great music from the heart. I started to believe in my life, hard as it often was."

Ludwig paused as he looked down.

"Go on Ludwig," encouraged the Countess pressing her hand into his.

"Well, look at me now! I am suffering from this blasted deafness, which seems to be getting worse, in addition to my ongoing poor digestion. The doctors can seemingly do nothing. When it looks like there is some hope and I get my spirits up, the deafness comes back with a vengeance, and I am beaten down again. Do you think this fair? The one sense I need, upon which I depend for my music, is the one I am losing!"

Ludwig's frustration and anger were increasingly dominating his tone of voice.

"Why am I not going blind instead, or losing my smell or taste? Why am I going deaf? Does my music displease Him? Is God punishing me? For what?"

Ludwig raised his hand above his head to remonstrate against the divine.

"I want him to know how angry I am at him. He is taking away my purpose in life!"

The Countess watched with great sadness, knowing, but now seeing in front of her, the depth of Beethoven's despair. She had been through this herself, alone.

"How can I trust Him again my dear? He shows me my destiny as a great composer, then goes back on His word by inflicting this on me. Without my hearing I will be like a fish out of water caught on a hook. I won't be able to hear my own music played! How am I going to make a living? I won't be able to hear your lovely voice either, nor the birds, nor anything in nature!"

Ludwig raised his hand in the air to damn the Almighty, but Anna Marie took it and pulled it down, gently. "Ludwig, Ludwig. Be still now."

She was about to say that she would be there for him and that they would go through this together, when

Ludwig just got up and turned his back on her. He stood there in silence not moving a muscle, eventually speaking in slow, deliberate words.

Anna Marie was apprehensive, and rightly so.

"Perhaps it would be better if I were dead," declared Ludwig. "The world wouldn't miss me. They already think I am nasty, mischievous, and mean-spirited. Maybe God does too!"

"No no no, they will miss you," Michael suddenly shouted out, startling JJ.

JJ thought the inspector was back from wherever he'd been. But just as unexpectedly Michael drifted off again.

Anna Marie felt tears come to her eyes. Somehow her pain and Ludwig's despair seemed the same. She went over to Ludwig and just took him in her arms, telling him to be still and not say a word. This had been what she had hoped her husband would do when in moments of intimacy she had turned away because of recurring pain.

Ludwig hugged her back. Suddenly he felt her own pain and disappointment, and knew how much she was giving of herself to support him. He felt embarrassed, even though this emotion was largely unknown to him.

"Tell me Ludwig, do you feel you have composed everything that you can?"

"Of course not," replied Ludwig in a surprised tone of voice.

"Then you must go on until you have. It's evident that both of us are called upon to drink from a sour cup and still find joy and fulfillment. I don't know how you are going to go on composing if you are deaf, but there you are. Perhaps you will be the first one ever to do so. I am still a married woman, Ludwig, but we shall find solace in each other, and in God. Somewhere, somehow, there is purpose here. You must not fail! "

The inspector seemed to stir again, as though moving in and out of some dream about Beethoven and his lady love and their purpose. What grabbed his attention was the importance of Beethoven being told he must not fail. Michael recalled a sermon he had once heard when it felt like it was being screamed into his ears and no one else's. He had realized that it had to do with him and not the preacher. Could the same be true now, he wondered?

The scene continued as Michael watched.

Ludwig was amazed. He had fallen in love many times before, as his beloved knew only too well, since he had told her. Something here was different. He had found courage to face the blackness and utter stillness that was creeping ever closer. In truth though, he knew that courage had found him through his beloved. He felt his luck improving, even if his increasing deafness might not be curable.

"I sense my dear, dear, dear Countess that I have been most selfish. I am sorry. Please forgive me."

"I do, Ludwig. I know you have just one mission, to write down your music, and that it drives you."

"That's only partially true, as you know, my love."

"We have been through this, Ludwig. You know it is not possible. In my position I must be discreet as well as being seen to be discreet, as well you know. My children's inheritance is at stake here."

As if it were yesterday, he recalled the dark day when he had kept his housekeeper but lost his beloved!

The inspector stirred again as though waking up from a vivid dream. This time he knew there was a correspondence with him and his wife.

Beethoven had truly offended his beloved because he had misread her motives in giving extra money to the husband of his domestic. He had not believed her when she had explained that she only wanted to free him from his constant spats with his servants and housekeepers. Beethoven's domestic had her own quarrels with him like all those before her. So to hurt him and get her own back she spread rumors that Beethoven's high and mighty aristocratic companion was really involved with her husband and paying him directly!

His beloved's response was seared into his memory:

"How could you have not believed me Ludwig? As if these rumors are not bad enough for one in my position, I cannot even rely on you—you to whom I have given my heart. How could you have believed for one second her dreadful lies that I cared anything for her husband? Were you so jealous and resentful that I have title and money from birth and you don't? Did your vanity blind you? And to make matters worse you still keep employing those same loathsome servants! Must I conclude that you side with them over me?"

I would like you to leave my house, Ludwig. That's the least you can do for me," and she walked away leaving Beethoven pawing over a gold ring.

♪

The inspector suddenly spoke out, his lips pursed, and his face showing a most determined look,

"Why are you so headstrong Ludwig? Apologize, apologize. She is your beloved, you love her." Michael recalled how his wife had walked out after their spat, when *he* had got on his high horse. JJ looked on as Michael drifted off yet again. Fr. Papandreou had told JJ not to wake him.

A shimmering effect occurred in the room followed by a change of scene.

♪

All the musicians and artists were inside the Great Temple to witness the work of discovery regarding the connections between colors and sounds in the brain. It was all about the Source's energy waves and their movements that create the world of form that was referred to as The Word of God. The ancient king was sitting in the high seat in the east to command the evening's work. He nodded to the chamberlain who promptly rose to his full height to begin directing the evening's proceedings of discovery. His voice was matter of fact and friendly, yet his commitment to truth was as clear as a shining star to those seeking more knowledge.

"Now, you twelve musicians are to sit here close together as a group. Starting with Aah, you will kindly intone each of the emotional sounds. You will draw each vowel sound out and sing each on the first note of our central scale. You will then repeat the same vowel sound on the next higher note in our scale until you have sounded one cycle for each of the vowels. The chamberlain will sound the first proper note and then you will repeat as I have directed."

They all nodded to the chamberlain and sat down.

"Now you twelve seers over here will act as observers tonight. You will sit in the west. You will look at the colors surrounding the heads of the first group as they intone one of the emotional sounds through the scale. You will then tell us on which note each intoned sound seems brightest, if any. This way we will know which emotional sound corresponds to which note and to which color. Please lower the lighting now so that it is very soft to the eyes. Let us begin!" The chamberlain bowed to the king and sat down.

"But first, our high chaplain will direct us in prayer to our creator and source that we may be successful in our endeavors tonight."

"Oh, great God and source of life and wonder, help to keep our thoughts and emotions positive and harmonious as we endeavor to learn how your world and universe is built up through numbers in such great harmony, from the dense through the less solid to the ethereal, to color and sound, one world in correspondence, Ah-men."

The king watched as the discovery began. Being one who was still born with full inner spiritual sight he could see the finer spiritual bodies, or "glories," of everyone as well as their level of being and understanding.

He wondered what else he could do, as slowly but surely His people were falling down the scale of "being," necessitating that this basic experiment be carried out every year to convince the lesser ones and the soldier class of the existence of a higher corresponding world that did the creating and from which they all sprang. Fortunately many in the soldier class still had their spiritual sight, so were still loyal to the king. But how long would it last?

The chamberlain gave further instructions.

"We shall now end by sounding the musical notes by themselves on our musical instruments and again seeing which colors you see when each note is sounded." And with that, the inspector sat down.

Of course, those of the pure and high would all see the same color corresponding to each note of the central scale. What was happening was that as the level of being and understanding was dropping and gradually being clouded over by limited sight and lowering emotions, there was no uniformity of perception and understanding any more. The archetype was being lost to individualism which was ascending, yet to good purpose.

The chamberlain rose for another demonstration.

"Now, you temple children here will hold hands and form a circle as big as you can. You will then all slowly walk in towards the center, stop for a while, and then come out again. You will repeat this several times and then speed up as fast as you can go. The temple lights will be extinguished so only the natural lights each of you is carrying will be visible."

You philosopher-seers will watch and observe as the children speed up their movements as they rush in and then rush out. Now proceed."

So, what have you noticed?" asked the chamberlain.

"Sir, when the speed of movement in and out is slow we can see everything, but when the movement is very fast our eyes can hardly follow, and we gradually end up only seeing the dense light at the center of the circle, which then looks like one light that is stationary and not moving."

The chamberlain rose to acknowledge this. "So, now you will understand that when the atoms in objects are vibrating very quickly they will be seen as seemingly stationary objects if we the observers ourselves are not vibrating at that speed or faster so as to follow the sensitive movements. The expansion or unfolding phase from the timeless zone that is followed by the folding in part of the cycle of all 'things' has been lost to many of our people who see or apprehend only the solid part. This we call 'The Fall.'"

Those of us who are of the 'higher' can still see this moving in and out, and we call this the field surrounding objects and people. It is the movement of the one in our world. This energy field around people tells us a lot about that individual. This is how our pure and ancient king can act as the ultimate judge of the realm. He can discern directly from any individual what he or she did or did not do. Those who have fallen are unable to perceive this radiation field and are limited, apprehending only the three dimensions of any solid object. Those of us of 'the higher' not only see what they see, but we see the level of being or complexity of that solid, and how much of the source's energy any individual is letting in."

Now I want you to go back to your respective districts and demonstrate this to the soldiers and lesser ones who come to your temples. This demonstration is to be part of the 'mysteries' program that will gradually help to raise the level of being of our 'lesser ones' back to 'the higher.'

You are to remember that we of the 'higher' are to serve the 'lower,' so that all are returned to the one." And with that, the evening's discovery program ended and the chamberlain sat down.

The inspector found himself looking down from on high, as though he was in his own attic. It seemed like he'd watched these scenes of Beethoven's life from upstairs where the composer's life and the lady he loved paraded before him. The depth of Beethoven's needs from his beloved was striking. But even more striking to the waking inspector was how he himself could have been so insensitive and blind in his own life, both with his father and his wife.

♪

"What are you doing, JJ?" asked the inspector as his boss tapped him on the shoulder to wake him up.

"You just kept on saying, 'With nothing but the will of God shall a man be concerned ... I will sing with knowledge, and all my music shall be for the glory of God ...'"

Michael said, "I have come down from some high place, like upstairs in my house, where I saw astonishing scenes and from where I seemed to look down on myself. The most remarkable thing, JJ! I saw Beethoven with his beloved, sometimes with others, and sometimes in his rooms all alone thinking about his tenth symphony and how we all need to change. That's his real message, that mankind needs to change, big time, just as he himself had to and learn to trust in the midst of despair. That's why these composers have thought the world was going to end. I must write this all down before I forget it. "

JJ was almost speechless. "Good heavens, Michael, are you serious? You're not kidding, are you? You're not deluded yourself now?" JJ wondered if anyone was going to believe this. But then he thought, I know one person who will definitely believe this, Fr. Papandreou.

"Listen, JJ, I remember someone telling me that they went to Stonehenge, and in those days stood with their back against one of the large stones while asking the question what went on there, and why. The man told me that he had had a vision of several men all dressed in white robes with golden headbands and then he saw a large pendulum swinging from the lintel between the tall stones. He said he just knew that this was used to predict the seasons and determine the length of the year. Of course I told him he was imagining it all. I thought he was one of these new age nuts prattling on about the sinking of Atlantis and how the Atlantean emigres had built Stonehenge after some went to Egypt and some to Albion. Now, with this new life-size replica of Stonehenge just having been built a little way away and, just as it was four thousand years ago, we know this is possibly true. Oh my, now look at me! Where is everybody, JJ?"

"Well, they left," I said. "You have been out of it for nearly one hour and more. I said I would look after you. Fr. Papandreou suggested not to wake you, but to let you wake up yourself, so I did just that, except when you started to say the same thing over and over again. You clearly have an ally in Fr. Papandreou. Lady Audrey nodded off as well, but I don't know any more. She and Sir Henry have gone back to their room now.

"You tell me what you saw and heard, Michael, and I will write it down as fast as I can. We'll then see what Sir Henry and Lady Audrey have to say."

JJ had a glimpse of the unique report that *The Times* would publish when this conference was over, confidentialities notwithstanding. He was about to hear of another recalling.

♪

Lady Audrey had stirred of her own accord. Sir Henry knew something had happened. He waited for his wife to speak.

"Henry, the most remarkable thing has just happened. I was watching Beethoven have all sorts of problems with his servants and landlords. What struck me was that not being married he did not have someone to take care of these things like I do for you Henry."

I also saw him at his lowest when his increasing deafness was leading him to nearly end it all. He thought he would not be able to have a life as a composer anymore, and was convinced that no one would respect a deaf composer, especially himself."

"That's certainly understandable, my dear. I wouldn't want to think how I would fare without you by my side, never mind being deaf too."

"Only this one remarkable lady, Henry, who gave him her heart, allowed him to survive his personal crisis in the early 1800s. She helped him to see that his musical genius could not be taken away from him since it was of the inner and not of the outer. So successful was her help that even when they quarreled and she was not around, he was still able to function."

Sir Henry was just going to speak about his wife's remarkable experience when Lady Audrey, looking straight into her husband's eyes, spoke softly to him, "But Henry, now what is troubling you? Are you afraid of losing something too?" She paused and watched him as he could not hide his emotions from his wife. "I know something is amiss with you. This 'mystery symphony' has touched you personally and deeply, almost wounding you. What is it? This is what I was thinking about when Fr. Papandreou asked us to join him in entering the silence."

She took her husband's hands into her own and just held them. She thought there must be something within her husband that resonated with the message in the 'mystery symphony.' Sir Henry's eyes filled with tears as he fought off his emotions.

"My dear," said Sir Henry. "I have never told you this but no man in my family has ever lived past sixty-five, and that will happen to me early next year as you know. Dr. O'Hara told me several months ago that I will most likely need a heart operation soon. I didn't tell you this. The message of annihilation in the 'mystery symphony' just reinforces it that my time is up." Lady Audrey pulled her husband to her and held him.

"Henry, how long have we been married and you never told me this? Now, lots of people have heart operations and very few die on the operating table. This is a childish fear of yours because it does not make any sense. You speak as though it's a done deal, a *fait accompli*, Henry.

I suppose that's the problem, because you are so true to your inner feelings and experiences, just like Beethoven was. You rise to great heights, but sink too, again like Beethoven. You know, Henry, sometimes common sense just can't get a word in edgewise with you.

Now, you said that rude inspector chap also nodded off and seemed to have experienced something. Maybe we can learn something from him here." They both started to walk slowly towards the hall to find Michael and JJ.

"Henry, do you think that every musician here thinks he is going to die soon? Surely not? Professor Stevens said that the real catastrophe would only happen to the earth about one hundred years in the future and that there was a fifty-fifty chance."

Sir Henry did not answer. JJ found them first as they approached, "Lady Audrey and Sir Henry, I am glad to see you both. The inspector, Mr. Lewis, has had the most amazing experience, assuming of course that he is not deluded himself now!"

Sir Henry smiled. "Well, Mr. Johnson, so has my wife, so let's forget the delusion. I am willing to forget that unfortunate outburst. There's obviously a lot more behind this 'mystery symphony' business. I can see this now."

The four of them sat down outside on the balcony of Sir Henry and Lady Audrey's room that looked out over the waters of the blue Mediterranean Sea. They gathered their thoughts, and exchanged experiences now that the inspector and Lady Audrey were literally 'back to their senses.'

The implications were staggering. They had both looked at the book of Beethoven's life. With his 'beloved immortal's help, Beethoven had found courage and survived the crisis of finding out that he was slowly going deaf and that there was probably no cure. Eventually letting go of his fear, at the same time that he went stone deaf, he started to live fully in his inner world of great creativity. Beethoven decided that if he could change on the inside so could everyone. His musical theme was 'the death of the old and the beginning of the new.' He started to write his tenth symphony on earth but only completed it in heaven. Joy of joy was his when he found out that his great suffering had cleaned his slate, and that he had found favor with God.

"Henry, did you hear that?" exclaimed Lady Audrey with confidence in her excited voice. "It's not God who wants to kill off mankind and the planet. Beethoven wrote it to tell mankind how much better the world would be if we would only get rid of some bad habits and stop running away from ourselves. Of course, he made it 'urgent' and 'imminent' in his typical fashion. How effective he was, too!"

Sir Henry nodded, yet struggling with this new "common sense information" that was really alien to him.

The inspector spoke as though delivering a lecture to immature first year students at his old police college, "What I observed was that when Beethoven accepted his growing deafness and let go, he became a new man on the inside. Seeing this as holy, he wanted to share it with mankind too—that change is possible."

For a brief moment it seemed that it made perfect sense that all had been solved, and so we could just go home. But then I watched as the inspector stood up and just blurted out, "My God, what has just happened? Look at us! We are so blasé, as though this happens every day. With all due respect, Sir Henry and Lady Audrey, we could all be going mad."

No one said anything. For JJ it was a bit scary. He thought maybe the inspector and Lady Audrey were indeed hallucinating, and that it was all nonsense. But then Sir Henry raised himself to his full height and, looking the part of the great conductor about to take charge of his orchestra in a splendid first movement, spoke: "Well, we must tell this to everyone tomorrow morning, and see what Fr. Papandreou and the clerics and Mr. Larson say about it. They deserve to hear about this."

And with this the four of them dispersed and went back to their respective rooms for a good night's sleep.

The inspector wondered, as he started to nod off, if what he had just experienced could happen again. He knew something—actually everything had indeed changed—and that Fr. Papandreou was the cause. His mind turned again towards Fr. Papandreou and Beethoven. This time he felt the rising like an updraft into the clouds. He imagined it might have been like this for Scrooge in Dickens's *A Christmas Carol* when he was told to hang on to the spirit as it moved upwards and onwards to show him what he needed to see.

♪

Inspector Lewis came to that night with scenes from Beethoven's life again in his mind, but it was more than this. He had come down from on high. For a brief moment he felt overwhelmed by these experiences. They were exceptionally real. He realized that he had felt entitled to have his former police career the way he wanted, irrespective of his superiors' wishes. He started to record again in his journal what he had experienced. Eventually he drifted back to sleep and got up the next morning as though everything was correct and normal. Yet he knew it was not. Where was it all going?

After breakfast the next morning Sir Henry joined Fr. Papandreou in welcoming all to the second day of their conference on the "mystery symphony."

"Ladies and Gentlemen, we ended yesterday's session with Fr. Papandreou inviting us all to join him in going into what he called 'the silence.' Well, I am here to tell you that to my knowledge at least two individuals did this with astonishing results. One was my wife, Lady Audrey, and the other was Mr. Lewis here. So I think we can forgive him his overzealousness yesterday. There is obviously a lot going on here, I think you will all agree."

Sir Henry paused to see if anybody else wanted to speak, but no one else showed any hint of wanting to get up, so he went on: "But first, Fr. Papandreou, would you like to comment yourself? After all, you started the ball rolling."

"Thank you, Sir Henry, but please let us hear from Lady Audrey and Mr. Lewis. I feel sure that we shall all benefit from hearing them first. After all, they are the ones who made the contact."

With that Fr. Papandreou sat down but without saying with whom or with what they had made contact!

Sir Henry spoke, "My dear, would you begin please?"

Then, turning to the audience, Sir Henry added, "I suggest we let Lady Audrey and Mr. Lewis both speak and tell their own tale. Our own questions and comments can follow."

With that, Lady Audrey stood up and recounted what she had seen and heard. The inspector did the same thing in a strictly matter of fact way. He knew what his colleagues at the Yard would say about him but he also knew what he had just experienced. Nobody said anything while they were talking. All were astonished, blown away really. Sir Henry invited Fr. Papandreou to comment, much to everyone's relief, since they were all still trying to swallow and take in what they had just heard.

"Well, Sir Henry, I am most glad about what I have just heard. We have learned now that the music was in a real sense written by Beethoven and that its purpose was to impart an important message to us. Second, it would seem that Beethoven's deafness facilitated compassion coming to him. Third, Sir Henry here no longer has the burden of believing that his life will be over soon. Now, Mr. Lewis, I suspect that you have benefited too, but I leave that to you."

The inspector was not ready to talk about himself. He needed time to reflect on his experiences. He normally investigated crimes and mysteries outside himself that were amenable to reason and his keen deduction. But now he would have to be the object of his own investigation. This he knew would require something outside of his normal self. But then that was what had just happened! Fr. Papandreou had obviously been instrumental in setting it up. The ball had started rolling, but where was it going? And what or who was pushing? The inspector had no answers except the bright light and violet streaks that he saw emanating from the good Father's head. He could hardly look at him. The light was so bright. It was clearly out of the ordinary. The only real question was if he was losing his mind! Yet he observed that Lady Audrey seemed not to be bothered by her experience. Rather she treated it as though she was just reading a book that recounted some of Beethoven's experiences.

I wonder if that is just how it is, thought the inspector, *like reading a book.*

Fr. Papandreou continued, "Apart from a sense of peace, I myself had no particular experience except that I was doing what I should be doing and tuning in to God's wavelengths."

JJ drew himself up to speak. He was thinking about how *The Times* newspaper would report this conference to its readers. He had given his word to Sir Henry and would not mention participants' names, nor the location of the conference. But to get the scoop that he wanted for the *Times*, some obvious questions had to be answered.

"Fr. Papandreou, if I may, this is astounding. This may be a common occurrence for you and the other clerics here, but I can see from the faces and reactions of our conductor friends that they are as perplexed as I am. There are many questions that come to mind."

What just happened to Lady Audrey and Mr. Lewis? Do you know? Is this normal or abnormal? What was your part in it? Did they really tune in to the past? If so, how did this happen?"

The inspector then stood up quickly to add, "And why did this Mr. Louis Beynon receive it, and no one else? Was he targeted? By the living, or by the dead?"

This last suggestion was shocking as it brought to mind for many of those present pictures of zombies following the living on the streets.

I wished the inspector had not said this. However, Fr. Papandreou ignored this, adding in a very matter of fact manner: "Let us not forget the question which bothered Mr. Beynon so much—did he talk to Beethoven in Heaven? If not, to whom was he talking?"

The Western Bishop could not contain himself any longer. "So now the walking dead are targeting the walking living and giving them ready-made symphonies, in this case written by Beethoven but not written down before he died. You must be joking! Where do you get this from? Even Mr. Lewis now sounds like he is losing it."

The conductors showed they found this difficult to swallow too! One of the Eastern clerics got up to speak. But before he could speak Sir Thomas stood up to take on again this Western Bishop, "My Lord Bishop, the inner hearing of ready-made orchestral pieces in the mind has been experienced before and by famous composers too, so any allusion to zombies and the like is uncalled for. Robert Schumann's wife testified that her husband heard the most beautiful music that was fully formed and complete. The music was glorious and said to be played on instruments that sounded more wonderful than those we have on earth."

"Yes, but didn't he go mad being plagued with hearing one note all the time? And isn't he supposed to have had syphilis too?" replied the Western Bishop, clearly pleased with his knowledge of 'their' subject.

"That occurred at the end of his life," replied Sir Thomas tersely. "He was most talented. Even as a child he could compose quite convincing melodies that picked up on his friends' traits and dispositions and which they all recognized and laughed at."

JJ remembered how his musical friends could do the same, and how accurate they had been in conveying the truth about his own truth or character. "So maybe music really can convey the truths of life and mankind," JJ mused."

Sir Henry gestured for the Eastern cleric to speak. He wanted to avoid any unnecessary confrontation, if possible. He understood well Sir Thomas's reaction to this sniping Western Bishop.

"Is the targeting of this Mr. Beynon so outlandish, my Lord? Let us look at Christian scripture here that has been the foundation of our civilization. We are told that the power of the Most High overshadowed Mary the mother of Jesus and the Holy Spirit came upon her leading to the virgin birth. Jesus, at his baptism, received the Holy Spirit and he then began his ministry. Are these not examples of two people being targeted quite specifically by God and His energies for the divine purpose in mind? And were the disciples of Jesus not targeted by Christ when they received the Holy Ghost at Pentecost? Was Saint Paul not targeted by the risen Christ to prepare him for his future work?"

The Western Bishop was quick on his feet again, "So now you are equating these dream-like experiences of Lady Audrey and Mr. Lewis here with Jesus himself, His

Holy Mother, and the holy apostles. Really! With all due respect to Lady Audrey here and Mr. Lewis—"

But he didn't have time to finish. Mr. Larson got up, and all turned to listen to what he was going to say.

"My Lord Bishop, surely everyone in tune with the finer and higher regions of life has access to these divine energies, according to their faith and practical need. Isn't this promised to us in the New Testament? It also seems clear to me that Fr. Papandreou established the connection with these higher regions, as he surely often does. I can imagine that he radiated his beautiful attunement to all of us in the room thanking God for the truth that would come to help us understand. We know that Lady Audrey had a clear, sincere, and heart-felt question in mind, and Mr. Johnson here has told me that few people are as committed to the truth as Inspector Lewis proved himself to be while at Scotland Yard, at great cost to himself. Getting clear answers to a question requires having understood the problem in clear and simple terms. So perhaps this is one reason why the 'lightning' went to them in particular. They were both active, prepared lightning rods, magnetized to receive."

The inspector suddenly remembered that he had seen that Beethoven kept a framed saying on his work desk. He blurted out, "Well, I think that Beethoven himself can help us here. He kept on his desk in a small frame the following saying written out in his own handwriting, *'I am that which is, I am all that was, that is, and that shall be. No mortal man hath lifted my veil. He is alone by himself, and to him alone do all things owe their being.'*

I believe that Lady Audrey and I made contact with his 'I am' and that Fr. Papandreou here made it possible."

The inspector sat down, having related his deduction in his normal, everyday calm way. He then realized what he had said. This may have seemed entirely obvious and logical to the inspector, Sherlock Holmes, and to Fr. Papandreou, but to those listening it was a stunning pronouncement. Everyone started to think of the "I am that I am."

There was absolute stillness. No one said a word or moved until Fr. Papandreou brought everyone back to earth. The room was pregnant with expectation. "If I read you correctly, Mr. Lewis you are still endeavoring to deal with your experience, a little like St. Paul after he was struck by the light on the road to Damascus."

The Western Bishop wanted to protest, but bit his tongue.

"You are right, Fr. Papandreou," said the inspector, rubbing his eyes. "But there are a couple of questions raised by Mr. Johnson here that we have not yet broached. Why did Louis Beynon get it, and was he indeed talking to Beethoven in heaven?"

With the good father's permission, Mr. Larson stood up to reply with obvious relish. "My grandfather taught that each human being is a whole world, an all, in effect a holographic image of the divine. The challenge is that like an iceberg, most of 'us' is below the water line of our awareness and so seems to be outside of us. We need to rise up Jacob's ladder or keyboard, discover who we really are, and be true to ourselves. We'll then be able to see how our expectations and actions help to create our future. This is where messengers or angels help us."

The voices that Louis Beynon heard most assuredly came to him through inner ears, albeit colored by his own experiences, so that he could recognize and then understand them. We know this is true because no one else heard the music and orchestra that he heard. So Louis Beynon connected with these finer inner levels of being, or if you like they connected with him, and the mystery symphony and voices were the result of that connection."

The inspector could hardly contain himself, "So what you are saying, Mr. Larson, is that what Lady Audrey and I experienced also came from within, through a connection to these finer, inner levels of life, just as my reasoning concluded, even if it was Fr. Papandreou who made it happen. Right?"

The inspector briefly wondered if it could happen now, away from Fr. Papandreou, since his own inner door had been opened. He saw himself investigating this, but was not ready to divulge it.

"Right, Mr. Lewis."

Although this had become a dialogue between the inspector and Mr. Larson, everyone, including all the clerics and the conductors, were on the edge of their seats, showing intense concentration.

"So then, Louis Beynon might not have been hearing Beethoven speak to him," said the inspector.

"In one sense that must be true, Mr. Lewis. After all, the physical body that was Beethoven disintegrated at his death."

"But I can tell you this, Mr. Larson," stated the inspector in an unusually confident tone of voice, "I saw that out of despair at losing his hearing as well as being so misunderstood, Beethoven felt driven to live deep within himself and away from this world."

Sir Henry got up now to support the inspector. "That is indeed correct, Mr. Lewis," said Sir Henry. "We know that in 1810 Beethoven recorded in his diary: '*Thus I can only seek support in the deepest, the most intimate part of myself; as for the external world, there is absolutely nothing there for me—no, nothing but injuries for me in friendship and feelings of the same genre.*'"

Mr. Larson stood up again, as if he had come to a definitive conclusion that warranted a pronouncement, "So, I think we can safely say that in the latter half of his life and certainly by 1827 when he passed on, Beethoven lived predominantly in his inner world rather than in the outer, just like we are when in a moment of utter concentration we suddenly come to, to be aware again of our outer circumstances. So, apart from losing his physical body or mortal coil, Beethoven in himself probably survived his physical death into the next world pretty much intact. So it is entirely possible that he could have contacted or overshadowed Louis Beynon later on with this 'mystery symphony;' if, of course, his intention received support from those higher up in the heavenly realms."

Up popped the Western Bishop. "Are you saying that he achieved 'salvation'? That is unbelievable."

"Well, maybe he did, my Lord Bishop," replied Mr. Larson. "But we really don't know. After all, to achieve salvation his inner self would have had to survive next the fire of the soul where everything not of goodness would have been burned away. Beethoven's great suffering in this world would have done a lot of this work for him while on earth. Perhaps his deafness helped him more than we know. Personally, I hope he did achieve salvation."

The Western Bishop bit his tongue. He could see that Sir Thomas and now the German conductors were getting ready to take him on. They had had enough of his constant sniping at Beethoven.

"But why was Louis Beynon the one to be targeted or the one to receive this musical message from on high?" The inspector had addressed his question to Mr. Larson, but Fr. Papandreou rose to reply.

"If I may, Mr. Lewis and Mr. Larson, we know several facts that may throw some light on this. First, I know that Louis and his mother and her family were devoted to the church and to God. Louis told me that he had prayed hard as a child and did his best to raise himself up to God and His truth. And as you heard me say before, I told Louis that perhaps this was God's reward coming to him. That is, Louis became able to create because the Creator had found him and so was able to express Himself through Louis. He had acquired a gift of the Holy Spirit!"

Second, there is the obvious fact that Louis Beynon was a professional musician but not a composer, and therefore able to write the music down that he heard in his head unaltered and without error. This he did successfully as we have all heard."

Third, he told me that his family believed that his father's relatives originally hailed from somewhere near Vienna. So it is possible that there is a genetic or inner relationship to

ERIK ERIKSSON

Beethoven here. Maybe Louis Beynon's ancestors are related to Beethoven's relatives. We just don't know here."

As Fr. Papandreou paused for a moment, JJ noticed that the inspector was gazing at him with concentrated attention.

"Wow, JJ, did Fr. Papandreou just say that Louis Beynon's ancestors could have been related to Beethoven? There may have been a child here that we know nothing about. Beethoven and the Countess were very close after she and her husband separated."

"Good Lord, Michael, have you been out there again? I saw that you seemed to be glued to every word that the good Fr. was saying."

Fr. Papandreou noticed that the inspector and JJ were in intense in their communication, as though something was about to happen over there.

"Mr. Lewis, if I may, am I right in saying that you made contact again?"

"I just experienced, Fr. Papandreou, that there may have been a child born from the love between Beethoven and his beloved. The child's name was Elise I think. I believe the Countess left Vienna to give birth to a girl who was then brought up by a relative on one of her foreign estates."

The conductors looked most surprised to hear this, and exchanged comments. Most smiled, thinking that it was quite on the cards since Beethoven had fallen in love many times. In fact, he was nearly always in love. They all knew Beethoven's famous bagatelle 'For Elise.' Some sniggered as though it was all true, recalling that Beethoven had kept a lot out of the public eye, not least for the Countess's sake.

Fr. Papandreou paused as though to wait, and then drew himself up to speak. If his demeanor was any indication, a change was in the air.

"Now, in a conference of this nature we also need to hear from science and especially medical science on phenomena of this nature. I was hoping that the New York neurologist Dr. Oliver Sacks would be able to attend in person, but this has proved impossible for him. He has, however, just e-mailed me his basic thoughts as well as some slides for us to look at. I will paraphrase his comments as well I can, and keep it short."

The conference heard that not so long ago many psychiatrists thought that anybody who heard inner voices must be mentally ill or psychotic. They were seen as living in some delusional state of complexes or psychoses in order to avoid having to deal with the outer world of the senses and its challenges.

Everyone could see in front of them that this was wrong. Fr. Papandreou was the perfect example of this error in official thinking since here right in front of their eyes was someone who had found "the peace that passes all understanding" and yet who was otherwise perfectly rational and 'normal.' Had not Jesus heard voices in his head too and had visions?

So Fr. Papandreou added that Beynon could not be said to be deluded on these grounds, even though Beynon had questioned his own sanity himself when he heard the Beethoven-like music in his head and the voice advising him what to do. In this regard, wasn't he like Jesus without the music?

The good Father gave out the latest research from Dr. Sacks and others, that when the five senses are quiet, this can trigger a 'backflow' from within the brain that is indistinguishable from normal sense perceptions, since the same circuits carry both types of signals. So music coming from within can sound like an orchestra playing in the room even though the recording has been turned off. Others in the room would of course hear no music playing at all.

A light came on in the inspector's head as he got up to speak.

"Father Papandreou, doesn't this mean that what is real to us is whatever we can realize, each individually? God is as real to the saint as are a coward's fears to a coward?" The inspector moved to sit down, but then got up again:

"We must be the captains of our own ship then."

"A most interesting conclusion Mr. Lewis, and timely. Thank you."

Dr. Klemper then stood up to speak, and was acknowledged by the abbot.

"Your excellencies, Sir Henry and Lady Audrey, the ability to direct and hear this inner music, (as all composers and musicians frequently do,) plus a heightened sensitivity, is surely what allowed Beethoven to go on composing after he went totally deaf." All the conductors nodded their agreement here including Sir Henry.

Fr. Papandreou resumed his summary of Dr. Sacks e-mail.

"So we may now add this Louis Beynon fellow to the list of those who have heard completely formed musical pieces in their heads. One difference from the other cases that Dr.

Sacks has investigated is that Mr. Beynon was able to write it down faithfully as he heard it, so that these musicians and conductors here could state, as he himself did, that this is Beethoven and no one else. Of course there can be no tangible proof of this. Yet these famous conductors here are all agreed, without exception, that this is Beethoven. The profound message in the music is, of course, another aspect. What triggered this experience in Louis Beynon may have been his devout love of God. But from what we have just heard the age-old religious practice of stilling the senses and the mind was likely the specific cause of this 'backflow' from within coming down to him."

The inspector was on a roll:

"Fr. Papandreou, you talked about angels and mentioned cases when there have been several people who have seen the same angel. Are these backflows too? Can you say more about this?"

"Well, one famous case involves your own fellow countrymen in the first world war. It has become known as 'the angel of Mons.' You might like to read up on these apparitions. An angel in the form of a female figure dressed in a long, white flowing gown with sandals on her feet, a golden headband, and white wings folded against her slim back appeared to a group of British soldiers of the Coldstream Guards. They had become separated from their main unit and were in danger of being annihilated by the encircling enemy. The soldiers first saw the angel in the form of a warm glow some distance in front of them. She then became more distinct and with her right hand started to beckon them to move out of the trenches they were digging and follow her along some path. When no one moved she drew closer and was more insistent. One by one they all moved out with their weapons and equipment and followed the glowing figure across an open field in complete silence. She led them to a halt on the upper rim of a sunken road, which an earlier patrol had not been able to locate. Raising her hand again, she led the way until all the soldiers had reached the end of the sunken road. She proceeded to float up the bank and pointed to a thicket of small trees a short distance away. She then turned, faced the soldiers, smiled a warm, pleasant smile at the amazed men, and vanished before their eyes. The soldiers soon made their way to the thicket where they encountered two British sentries of a forward observation post of their main unit. The British High Command had written them off. Neither map nor any local resident knew or had any evidence of the road they had taken that had saved their lives. Retracing their steps a few days later no sign of that road was ever located. Most interestingly, the soldiers reported that the angel resembled a drawing of one of the angels depicted in their regimental chapel."

"Well, I certainly thank you," said the inspector, squinting again at the good Father. "That is incredible. Being visible to many of the soldiers certainly made it more likely that they would all follow and thereby escape destruction. From what we have just heard, it would seem that this 'visual back flow' would have been brought about by a desperate cry for help that effectively shut out their outer world for long enough to protect them and save their lives."

The inspector suddenly wondered if a similar back flow led Moses to see the burning bush. Or was this how things looked when you could see more than just the dense physical?

Fr. Papandreou had been reading the inspector's thoughts here:

"If I may, Mr. Lewis, I think you are forgetting how a person's life is changed when God's spirit comes to them. Perhaps you will remember that after his talk with God on Mount Sinai, Moses shone with such an extraordinary light that the people were not able to look at him. He was forced to wear a veil when he appeared in public."

Likewise when Jesus was transfigured on Mount Tabor, a great light encircled him. St. Mark says that 'His raiment became shining, exceedingly white like snow, and His disciples fell on their faces from fear.'"

So you see, Mr. Lewis, those who see light are within the light, and share the brilliance of light. Just so, those who see God are within God and receive of His splendor, a radiance of the vision of God that gives us life."

The inspector could see the bright light surrounding the good Father but had not yet realized that what the abbot said applied to him. Fr. Papandreou knew he would need to be more direct to accomplish his goal.

"This is all very well, Fr. Papandreou, but how can we know if we are living in the Spirit of God?" the inspector retorted.

What happened next raised everybody's eyebrows, conductors and clerics alike.

The discourse was over. Things were about to get personal. The question was what biblical drama was about to begin, and who was in the play?

Fr. Papandreou stepped down from the stage and walked right over towards the inspector. There was amazement in the air. What was he going to do? The good Father suddenly took the inspector very firmly by the shoulders, "Look at me, Mr. Lewis."

"I cannot look, because light is flashing from your eyes. Your face has become very bright. It makes my eyes ache."

"Don't worry about that," said the good Father.

And with that I saw the inspector look straight at Fr. Papandreou.

"Now you yourself are as bright as I am. You are now in the fullness of the spirit of God yourself; otherwise you would not be able to see me as I am," replied Fr. Papandreou.

And just as suddenly as the inspector had looked straight into the good Father's eyes did the strength in his legs seem to leave him. JJ instinctively put out his hands thinking that the inspector might fall. It looked as though he had seen too many of those religious shows on TV when the candidates on stage were gently pushed into the arms of waiting helpers by the ministering evangelist.

But he hadn't been pushed, and this wasn't TV.

A few seconds later when the inspector had recovered, Fr. Papandreou again looked him in the eye. "Well, Mr. Lewis, now that you know what it is to be in God's Holy Spirit, tell me, what's it like, how do you feel?"

The inspector did not respond straightaway. JJ wondered if he was all right.

"I feel really well, peaceful; like there is no time, I just am. There is a beautiful melody I can hear and a spectrum of beautiful colors. It sounds like it's the very wellspring of my life; but one phrase stares out at me, as though I beat to its drum."

"Ah, I see that you are in tune now, and you understand, Mr. Lewis," said the good Father. The beautiful melody corresponds to the harmony and hum of God's creative 'Word' that goes out in perfect rhythm and creates the world, sustaining everything in it, and at all levels down to ours. That musical phrase corresponds to your inner self, which transmits it outwards. It is what specifically motivates you, what inspires you and excites you to do what you are here to do."

You now know that time really stands still and does not move; that we are ever-living and moving in the great eternal now of the creator."

The inspector suddenly took on a bewildered look. All things were apparently not understood.

"You will discover, Mr. Lewis, that whatever you ask for while in this connected state that is for the glory of God or for the good of your neighbor you will receive or be able to accomplish. 'You being in the light,' this is what I prayed for just now, and look how it was answered."

"But Fr. Papandreou, how can it be that there is no time?"

"Well, when we look up in the sky we see the sun moving across the sky and we seem to be stationary, right? But of course it is we on the earth who are moving around the sun. Galileo was right. So it is that we are moving through the great eternal now of inner space, around the source or God.

It is movement that gives rise to time. This is what the great Newton knew, who was incidentally devoted to God."

The good Father explained how Newton saw the correspondence between us moving through inner space round God, and the planets orbiting the Sun. This quickly led him discovering to the law of gravitation.

"We have all the time we need and so do you, Mr. Lewis, for all your questions to be answered. The more you concentrate, the more will you know this to be true."

Not all the conductors and clerics could readily hear and see what was transpiring near the inspector and JJ, but they all knew something extra-ordinary was afoot. Fr. Papandreou went back to the podium to speak.

"Well, my prayers have been answered. I told you before that I knew that Mr. Lewis had to be here. Not only has he, with Lady Audrey, been instrumental in finding out for us about the source of this 'mystery symphony,' but now he himself has reconnected with the spirit of God. It was his time."

There is only one further comment I wish to make and that of course relates to the warning in the 'mystery symphony' itself. I do believe the safety of our world is in our hands as well as God's. If enough of us make the effort to reconnect with our loving Creator, or at least do our best to live positive and caring lives, then the catastrophe may be averted. If not, then our world and species may suffer what we have heard has happened several times in our planet's past; clearly so that those who come after us may be more successful regarding God's dream of knowing Himself and all that He has created through us."

This was too much for the Bishop who objected to music being able to convey such information. He related to words and the Bible. He had never experienced the sublime beauty of a piece of music that could bring you speechless to its altar. To JJ's music friends he was another philistine.

"But Fr. Papandreou, how can this be? The Bible does not tell us this?"

"That is true my Lord, but the Bible does tell us about Noah and one flood. And we know from the words of the disciples themselves that Jesus did many more things than are recorded in the Bible. So we must not see the Bible as a history book of our planet. I am sure you will agree, my Lord."

The Western Bishop genuinely agreed.

"Well, there are many ways to finding the kingdom of heaven. Devotion to God and the religious life is one of them, but science is clearly another, as is the love of beauty that inspires poets and artists such as Beethoven or William Blake. Wasn't Einstein blessed by God to discover from science and mathematics that time is relative? The saints discovered this themselves as they came closer and closer to God in their inner space! There can be no lasting differences between faith and science, since they complement each other, looking as they do at different aspects of our one world. What is needed is an honest heart that tries to understand the world, as does a baby learning to crawl and walk. When major differences or confrontations seem to arise, we can be sure that we are missing something, or that we need to look again at our motives or our undeveloped side. Even evolution in the natural world does not contradict God's truth. Are we not all ourselves slowly evolving so as to adapt better to this world to gain a mastery over its laws? Forms may come and go, but then form is just that! The spiritual difference comes when as individuals we choose to do it faster through faith."

If there are no further questions, then I think we shall bring these sessions to a formal end. We can now have a bite to eat and discuss amongst ourselves as we wish."

And with these words the conference was formally closed. JJ was flabbergasted, dumbfounded would be an understatement. Clearly Lady Luck had had its eye on the inspector for some time. JJ realized that you can never know everything about a person from looking at the outside. The caterpillar seems dead in its chrysalis, but when the caterpillar breaks out you can see that it had transformed itself into something else. So if the caterpillar could do this, thought JJ, couldn't mankind?

JJ made a mental note to himself to read up on the Angel of Mons and to talk to his wife Angela and her military relatives when he and the inspector got back to England. This was part of military history and could not be so easily dismissed. This scientific back flow business was intriguing, not just because it felt right, but because it came from medical research. But hearing that the Word of God had an equivalent musical phrase or melody that created and sustained the world was to say the least memorable. JJ thought about Joshua bringing down the walls at Jericho. He would never look at the piano keyboard in the same way again.

Before retiring to bed that night the inspector decided to follow Fr. Papandreou's advice once more and to use the good Father's words, "commune." He would put it to the test and see what "back flow" he would get on his own.

"You know, JJ, I sat down and relaxed into a comfortable chair in my room, turning my thoughts to Fr. Papandreou and the rays of bright light that I saw emanating from his head."

When I came to, I was aware of Fr. Papandreou at an altar. My spirit was now with others in what looked like some heavenly temple in inner space. I saw his hand move up and down over the altar as though he was getting ready to give a blessing. Then, suddenly, violet light flashed from between his hand and the altar and hit me right in the middle of the forehead. The jolt of it is surely what sent me right back to my body waking me up. As I came to, I then heard music, beautiful clarinet music, just like my father used to play. It was in color and spoke to me. My father and I were finally at peace. I was renewed, although to the casual observer, little would be seen as different."

Michael told me that he was aware that many of his colleagues would see him now as credulous, but he wasn't overly concerned. He knew he had been changed for the better, and that was what counted. But what would he do? I knew he would pursue it further. Somehow I started to see him as the apostle to the English, a new "steward of the mysteries."

But would he and the others be in time? I recalled Fr. Papandreou's comments about the earth. What would the future unfold?

The Future Arrives Out of the Blue

The year 2012 had come and gone, and Louis Malcolm and his bride Marie were thoroughly enjoying the second week of their honeymoon in the Azores. Louis had just finished recording a series of piano concertos in London while Marie was beginning her career as a soprano at Covent Garden. Both were graduates of The Royal Academy of Music where they had met and fallen in love. They had flown to the islands in the Atlantic from Madeira where they had spent their first week.

"I am going jogging near Mt. Pico darling," said Louis as he tied up the laces on his latest running shoes.

"Ok, sweetie," replied Marie warmly as she opened up a tourist book on the islands. She was looking at a map of the

Mid-Atlantic Ridge from Iceland in the north through the Azores to Tristan Da Cunha in the south. To her surprise, the ridge seemed to go right under where she was sitting.

As he turned on his wristwatch radio, Louis set off running towards Mt. Pico in the distance. Radio stations from all over the world came on to give him their fifteen second offerings in the latest holographic 3-D sound that was audible to him without any earphones, but to nobody else, even those who might be standing close by.

As one radio station was selected, the last movement of Beethoven's ninth symphony filled his hearing space. He didn't recognize the recording but liked what he heard. As the glorious voices faded away and the piece ended, he turned off the radio and just watched the sky near Mt. Pico, enjoying the uplifting scenery.

As was his normal practice, Louis had pressed the record button on his watch so that when he got back Marie could hear his spoken thoughts and any creative ideas that often came to him on his runs. He quickly found his natural rhythm of running, which made every-thing harmonious and graceful. He relaxed into his stride.

"Wow, look at those sky colors. They're continu-ously changing their hues. There are people climbing up towards the top of Mt. Pico. And now there's music."

Well, darling, I am now listening to this powerful symphony on the radio, ominous stuff really, sounds like Beethoven, but nothing I can name, which is weird. I've recorded it so you too will be able to hear it when I get back. It reminds me here and there of the last movement of Beethoven's ninth. There's also the suggestion of parts of the Choral Fantasia."

Well, as you'll hear, it was heavenly to start off with, but now, well, it's as if we've all been found wanting and we're to be sentenced soon."

Louis heard the scherzo end on a long, drawn out shriek of agony. It made him think that some terrible decision had been made.

"My God, this slow movement sounds like a requiem for us. There's a nothingness, an agonizing stillness, as if over eons of time. Now sopranos are beginning a plea that man be given another chance, but the judge summarily dismisses this. He says he has been through this before."

As Louis redirected his attention to the top of the peak to free his mind from this dreadful nothingness in the music, a shimmering effect seemed to pass by.

♪

Louis was next to a young man dressed in white. He had a golden headband and was walking steadily with him in a procession towards the top of the peak. He knew that one path was called 'At-one-ment' and that the other processional line was named 'Discovery,' a combination of science and religion that comprised the two pillars of wisdom.

As he turned round the next corner near the top Louis heard a voice address him.

"Keep moving please. We must be there in good time for the ceremony."

"You know, young man, there is a rumor that we are all going up to the temple too late. Some are saying that the One has already unfolded his decision to the king and council and that it's just the soldiers who won't listen."

"I don't know anything about that, sir," replied the man to Louis. "I wouldn't pay any attention to that if I were you. The warriors are controlling the shots now."

We arrived in the supreme temple just as the ceremony was beginning.

"How can it be too late?" said the young man. "The sun is right on time between the pillars as normal."

"I don't know, but I can tell you that something is wrong."

Louis's thoughts were poignant.

These men are not the normal temple custodians. They are not performing the ritual properly. They are supposed to wait until after the king speaks the royal sound for the attunement message to come through before doing that.

Louis moved away. He knew his worst fears had come true. There had been a changing of the guard. He doubted the king was still alive. He thought he had probably been dispatched along with the staff in the supreme temple.

"Where are you going sir?" asked one of the outer temple guardians as I left.

"I am not well and need to rest and then go home," said Louis.

"Very well, pass."

Louis was discreet in making his way home to his wife. As they embraced, his wife knew something was seriously wrong.

"My dear, we must pack and leave. What I heard the other night must be true. I doubt that our king and council are still with us. Eventually the truth will come out. We can travel by land and tell the sentries that we are going to see our relatives on the other side of the island for a visit. Then we must take a ship to one of our colonies, like Albion or Egypt. We shall be welcomed there. It is time to leave here before the calamity arrives."

♪

The shimmering passed over and Louis was back in his stride having turned the corner about to arrive back at their hotel.

Louis ran into the hotel and saw Marie sitting by the heated pool, looking as calm and beautiful as ever.

He could hardly contain himself , never mind catch his breath.

"Darling, darling, you'll never believe what happened on my run. I was listening to this awesome, but frightening music that was on the radio. I recorded it with my comments as it played. And then it was suddenly like I was back in antiquity walking into a temple as they were experimenting with sounds and colors. And then, well, we escaped before the calamity arrived."

"Louis slow down, slow down. Now tell me what happened."

Louis described to Marie the music on the radio, and then what happened and what he had heard and seen.

"Well, let's hear the music, Louis, along with your comments."

Louis pressed the recall button. His comments were there loud and clear, but there was no music.

"Well, where is it Louis? Did you imagine it or what?"

"Don't be silly, darling. I first heard Beethoven's ninth symphony, actually the last movement, and then this awesome Beethoven-like symphony came on a little later. It was terrifying in places. It ended as though God had pronounced His final judgment on mankind, the extinction of our species. It felt like it was just round the corner."

"Well, where is it then?" said Marie as she still sipped her drink. "Think, Louis. What do you remember doing?"

"I remember turning off the radio when Beethoven's ninth ended. So how did the radio come on again?"

'Well obviously you turned it on again and you've forgotten!" said Marie.

"No, no, now I remember. Oh my God! Wait, I have heard this before somewhere."

"What's come over you?"

Louis hesitated a while before speaking. "You don't know what it is. Now I know. It's called the 'mystery symphony,' written about a hundred years ago. My great uncle, Sir Henry Malcolm, knew the composer and in fact conducted the first performance of it in London."

"What's all the mystery about then?"

"Well, you see, the composer, a chap named Beynon, died and never actually heard the first performance, a bit like Beethoven and his ninth symphony; but there was an air of mystery about it because there were rumors and goodness knows what that he never actually composed it but was given it from above, from the spirit world, sort of telepathy or being overshadowed I think they call it. I used to think it a lot of nonsense until my father told me what great uncle Sir Henry had told him about its origin. In any event Louis Beynon heard it in his head and wrote it down. Even he said he did not compose it but got it from on high or from within. They all agreed it was Beethoven. It's wonderful music I know, but I must confess it disturbs me and I might say frightens me a bit," Louis replied.

"Why ever should it frighten you, darling? I've never known you to be upset by music."

"All right, love. I'll tell you. Dad, when he told me this, said I was to keep it to myself. You see, Sir Henry was quite satisfied that not only was this music composed by Beethoven who had been dead nearly 180 years then, but that it was given to Beynon through some … well … supernatural means."

"But how silly, Louis, surely you didn't believe him?" said Marie.

"Wait a minute, now. Sir Henry called a meeting of all sorts of experts in addition to the greatest conductors of the day. I understand the conference was successful and concluded that the music had indeed been written by Beethoven. But the point is that Sir Henry said that the music contained a dire warning that destruction was just around the corner, and by extraterrestrial means. *The Times* published the conference results and it became quite the talking point for some time. My great uncle met with a famous physicist of the day and was told of a comet coming close to Earth that would in all likelihood cause devastation."

"What then?"

"Well, darling, it's just about that time now, and for some reason every time we have floods, tsunamis, and earthquakes, I know it's silly, but my mind goes back to the so-called warning in the music. Also, just after that performance in London, they had terrible floods in England, raging summer fires in Greece and California, and then massive floods in Asia. Nobody wanted to hear the music anymore after that. Most found it quite unnerving. In fact, my dad said that there were only a few more performances of the 'mystery symphony' after that and then no more. All the copies of the music that my great-uncle gave out were faithfully returned to him and the symphony just disappeared out of sight, causing more mystery."

"That's a nice story, Louis, but how do you know it's got anything to do with the music you heard today?"

"Because I am starting to hear it again. Now I recognize it. I've heard it before. You can't hear it, can you?"

"There's nothing to hear darling," retorted Marie, acknowledging she couldn't hear anything.

"No wonder it wasn't recorded then! The music is in my head!" said Louis. "I've obviously inherited it from my father and Sir Henry."

"Oh my, you've got to be kidding, Louis. You're not sick are you? I have heard about this, of course. Let's go for a walk on the beach. It'll help to clear your head."

Hand in hand they strolled down to the beach and the lagoon, perfectly happy in their mutual affection but now perturbed by this unexpected musical mystery. The moon was rising and seemed to light up the tops of the clouds presenting a long silver line just above the horizon. They heard thunder and lightning off to the east as a huge white streak in the sky appeared as though shooting stars had exploded. Then, as Marie stepped into the canoe, she stumbled. "Good heavens, I thought the ground moved then, didn't you, Louis?"

"Yes, I did, but I thought they haven't had earthquakes here for some time."

Once in the canoe they quickly moved off on the calm water thoroughly enjoying the peaceful atmosphere.

"Oh, look Louis," said Marie. "Isn't that a silver lining on the clouds over there where the storm is? But it seems to be shimmering and moving closer; funny, isn't it?"

The waters of the lagoon started jerking about, swelling into a seething mass.

"Oh my God," said Louis, "it's not a cloud we're looking at. It's a huge wave moving towards us at a hell of a lick. Come close darling, quickly. This looks like the big one. I can hear that 'mystery symphony' again."

"So can I now Louis, we are joined in music too. I love you forever," replied Marie.

The shimmering did not pass over again.

The mid-Atlantic ridge was slowly moving upwards carrying Atlantis with it, and another earth change was on the way.

Epilogue

Meanwhile, somewhere in the upper registers of life's keyboard, the inspector and his dad are taking music lessons from the master in preparation for their return to earth and their chosen new family.

There is much preparation and thinking to be done if he and his dad are going to succeed in their new mission on earth as stewards of life's mysteries. Michael knows that earthly life has a habit of clouding over the best laid plans made in heaven. He had seen how this had recently happened with himself.

As the music class ended, the inspector's thoughts turn to the power of prayer and love and how this will allow them to keep in touch when they are back in an earthly body. Straightaway as his thoughts changed, he sees Kahlil Gibran who is holding forth "nearby" on these topics from his book *The Prophet*. Michael listens enraptured, only to prove to himself that great truth: "As a man thinketh in his heart, so is he."

Michael decides that perspective is everything. In his upcoming mission he and his father will teach people when they love to say: "I am in the heart of God," rather than "God is in my heart." As he says this, his own perspective is suddenly brought into sharp focus as his attention is shifted to the blinding light and beauty above him in the higher realms. Seemingly at the same time, the word sounds forth, and an irresistible chord pushes him downwards to Earth's realm, to the world of space and time.

He will shortly have a new father and mother, so he vows he will not forget his real home. Yet he knows that his future earthly self will surely exercise its freedom and take on a life and identity of its own. So he decides to make it a law of his psyche, that whenever he is in danger of forgetting that he really lives in the Light, in the heart of God, the mystery symphony will sound off with its story and warning of destruction. Beethoven's Tenth will announce once again the end times of Earth's domination of another human soul.

"The tests and trials of life are not to break us but to make us."

"But if it takes not place in me, what avails it? Everything lies in this, that it should take place in me."

The Heiligenstadt Testament

WRITTEN BY
LUDWIG VAN BEETHOVEN IN 1802

For my brothers Carl and _____ Beethoven.

O you men who consider, or describe me as quarrelsome, peevish, or misanthropic, how greatly you wrong me! You do not know the secret reason why I seem to be so. From my childhood onwards my heart and soul have been filled with tender feelings of goodwill, and I have always been willing to perform great and magnanimous deeds.

But reflect for the past six years I have been in an incurable condition made worse by unreasonable doctors. From year to year I have hoped to be cured, but in vain, and at last I have been forced to accept the prospect of a permanent infirmity (whose cure may perhaps take years, or may prove to be quite impossible.) Although born with a fiery and lively temperament, and even fond of the distractions of society, I soon had to cut myself off and live in solitude. When occasionally I decided to ignore my infirmity, ah, how cruelly I was then driven back by the doubly sad experience of my poor hearing, yet I could not find it in myself to say to people: "Speak louder, shout, for I am deaf." Ah, how could I possibly have referred to the weakening of a sense which ought to be more perfectly developed in me than in other people, a sense which I once possessed in the greatest perfection, to a degree which certainly few of my profession possess or have ever possessed. I cannot do it, so forgive me if you see me withdraw from your company, greatly though I should like to mix with you.

My misfortune afflicts me doubly as I am bound to be misunderstood. For me there can be no relaxation in human society, refined conversations, and mutual confidences. I must be entirely alone, and except when the utmost necessity takes me to the threshold of society I must live like an outcast. If I appear in company I am overcome by acute anxiety, for fear I am in danger of revealing my condition. Such has been the case this last half year, spent in the country, instructed by my sensible doctor to spare my hearing as much as possible, which is indeed my present inclination.

Sometimes I have been driven by my desire to seek the company of other human beings, but what humiliation when someone, standing beside me, heard a flute from afar off, while I heard nothing, or when someone heard a shepherd singing, and again I heard nothing! Such experiences have brought me close to despair, and I came near to ending my own life—only my art held me back, as it seemed to me impossible to leave this world until I have produced everything I feel it granted to me to achieve. So I continue this miserable existence—truly miserable, as my body is so sensitive that my condition can change rapidly from very good to very bad. Patience—that must be my guide, as I am determined, and I hope will always remain so, to endure until it pleases the inexorable Parcae to break the thread. Perhaps my lot will improve, perhaps not—at the age of twenty-eight I was compelled to become a philosopher. It has not been easy, and more difficult for an artist than for anyone else. Oh God, you look down on my inner soul, and know that it is filled with love of humanity and the desire to do good. Oh my fellow men, when you read this someday, reflect that you have done me wrong, and let him who is unfortunate comfort himself with the thought that he has found someone equally unfortunate who, despite all the burdens placed on him by nature, did all which was in his power to earn a place among worthy artists and human beings. You, my brothers Carl and—, as soon as I am dead, if Professor Schmidt is still living, ask him in my name to describe my disease, and add the paper I have written here to the documents of my illness, so that after my death the world will be reconciled with me as far as possible. At the same time I hereby nominate you both as my heirs to my little property (if it can be so called;) share it honestly, live in harmony, and help each other. You know that the harm you did me has long since been forgiven. I thank you, brother Carl, in particular, for the goodness you have shown to me of late. My wish is that your lives will be better and less care-laden than mine. Urge your children to follow the path of virtue, as that alone can bring happiness—money cannot. I speak from experience as virtue alone has sustained me in my misery, and it was thanks to virtue, together with my art, that I did not end my life by committing suicide. Farewell, and love one another. I thank all my friends, especially Prince Lichnowsky and Professor Schmidt. I wish Prince Lichnowsky's instruments to be kept safely by one of you, but do not make them an occasion for strife between you; as soon as they can serve you in a more useful way, sell them—how happy I shall be if, in my grave, I can still be of use to you both! So be it, I go joyfully towards death. If it comes before I have had the chance to develop all my artistic abilities, that will be too soon for me, despite my hard fate, and I would wish it to be postponed—yet should I not be satisfied, would it not release me from a condition of endless suffering?

Come, when you will, death, I will meet you resolutely. Farewell, and do not entirely forget me when I am dead; I have deserved to be remembered by you, as I have often thought of you during my lifetime. May you be happy.

—Ludwig van Beethoven
Heiligenstadt, 6th October 1802

Schiller's Ode to Joy

O friends, no more these sounds, let us sing more
cheerful songs, more full of joy (Beethoven's words.)
Joy, bright spark of divinity, Daughter of Elysium,
Fire-inspired we tread Thy Sanctuary.
Thy magic power re-unites all that custom has divided,
All men become brothers under the
sway of thy gentle wings.
Whoever has created an abiding
friendship or has won a true and loving wife,
All who can call at least one soul theirs
join in our song of praise;
But any who cannot must creep
tearfully away from our circle.
All creatures drink of joy at nature's breast.
Just and unjust alike taste of her gift.

BEETHOVEN'S TENTH SYMPHONY

177

She gives us kisses and the fruit of the
vine. A tried friend to the end.
Even the worm can feel contentment,
and the cherub stands before God!
Gladly, like the heavenly bodies
which He set on their courses
Through the splendour of the firmament;
Thus brothers you should run your race
as a hero going to conquest.
You millions I embrace you.
This kiss is for all the world!
Brothers, above the starry canopy
there must dwell a loving father.
Do you fall in worship you millions?
World, do you know your creator?
Seek Him in the heavens!
Above the stars must He dwell."
—Friedrich Schiller, 1785

Bibliography

"Ludwig van Beethoven." (Edited by Joseph Schmidt-Görg and by Edmund Morris), Deutsche Grammophon Gesellschaft MBH. Hamburg; Polydor International GmbH, Hamburg, 1972.

"Beethoven's Beloved" by Dana Steichen: Doubleday and Company Inc., Garden City, New York, 1959.

"The Beethoven Encyclopedia" by Paul Nettl, Carol Publishing Group, New York, 1994.

"Beethoven's Letters" by Dr. A.C. Kalischer; Dover Publications Inc., New York, 1972.

"Beethoven—The Universal Composer" by Edmund Morris: Harper Collins Publishers, New York, 2005.

"Beethoven—The Master Musicians" by Frederick J. Crowest: London, J. M. Dent & Co. 1899.

"Beethoven the Composer as Hero" by Philippe Autexier: Thames and Hudson, London (Translated by Carey Lovelace), 1992.

"Beethoven—His Spiritual Development" by J.W.N. Sullivan: Vintage Books, New York, 1927.

"Musicophilia—Tales of Music and the Brain" by Dr. Oliver Sacks: Alfred A. Knopf, New York, 2007.

"Secrets of the Hidden Scrolls" by Ben Finger, Reprinted from the Rosicrucian Digest, Vol. 34, No. 10, (October 1956), pages 368–371 in Rosicrucian Digest No. 2, Web Supplement, 2007.

"Time Warps" by John Gribbin: Delacorte Press/Eleanor Friede, New York, 1979.

"A time and times and the dividing of time"; Sir Isaac Newton, the Apocalypse and 2060 A.D" by Stephen D. Snobelen: Canadian Journal of History, Vol. XXXVIII, December, 2003. www.isaac-newton.org/newton_2060.

"Napoleon Bonaparte" by Alan Schom: Harper Perennial/ Harper Collins Publishers, New York, 1997.

"The Way of a Pilgrim" (Translated from the Russian by Mrs. Eleanor French): Harper Collins, New York, 1965.

"The Power of Positive Thinking" by Norman Vincent Peale: Simon and Schuster, New York, 2003.

"The Book of Mystical Chapters—Meditations on the Soul's Ascent from the Desert Fathers, and Other Early Christian Contemplatives" (Translated and Introduced by John Anthony McGuckin: Shambhala, Boston and London, 2003.

"The Prophet" by Kahlil Gibran: Wordsworth Editions Ltd., Ware, Hertfordshire, U.K 1996.

"Story Structure Architect" by Victoria Lynn Schmidt Ph.D:Writers Digest Books, Cincinnati, Ohio, 2005.

"Reading Like a Writer" by Francine Prose: Harpers Collins Publishers: New York, 2006.

"On Creativity" by David Bohm: Routledge, London and New York, 2004

"Wholeness and the Implicate Order" by David Bohm: Routledge and Kegan Paul, London and New York, 1980.